Returning Injury

A Suspense Celebrating Women's Strength

by

Becky Due

TELEMACHUS PRESS

The publisher does not have any control over and does not assume any responsibility for author or third-party websites or their content.

Cover art and design by Craig Van Wechel Design

Published by Telemachus Press, LLC
http://www.telemachuspress.com

Visit the author website:
http://www.BeckyDue.com

Library of Congress Control Number: 2012948305

ISBN: 978-1-938701-50-4 (eBook)
ISBN: 978-1-938701-51-1 (Paperback)

Version 2012.09.11

Printed in the United States of America

10 9 8 7 6 5 4 3 2 1

Returning Injury

A Suspense Celebrating Women's Strength

Sunday
3:00 PM

REBECCA WAS IN a hurry. She had been cleaning out files the last few days, trying to better organize her office, because she planned to throw herself into her work for the four days Jack would be out of town on business.

"Honey," Jack hollered, "it's three o'clock."

"I'm coming," she yelled back, grabbing a stack of old folders that she still needed to go through and hurrying to slip them into a drawer. The bottom folder slid across the desk and onto the carpet, spilling its contents across the floor. "Ugh!"

She picked up the first thing she saw. It was a small card in an envelope, like the kind that comes with flowers. On the front of the envelope was a fancy R. She knew exactly who it was from and when she had received it. Her heart started racing. Wondering why she still had it, she opened it and read, To: Rebecca, An Angel in my Heart. From: Roy.

Jack peeked into her office. He was a clean cut, handsome man with brown hair and brown eyes. He was in shape with meat on his bones, and looked great in his jeans. Rebecca thought he was the sexiest man alive, and no matter what he was wearing, he always looked like somebody important, somebody who wore a suit for work. "You ready, honey?"

"Yeah."

"You okay?"

"Yeah, yeah, I'm fine. Distracted. I have a lot of work to do." She tossed the card upside down on the papers lying on the floor.

"Well, you won't have me around bugging you for four full days," he smiled.

Rebecca smiled back, grabbed her bag and gave him a quick peck on the lips. "I'll miss you."

"Sure you will." He gave her a big hug. "You love it when I go out of town."

"… but I still miss you." Rebecca did like it when he left town. The house was always clean. She did what she wanted when she wanted. She worked when she wanted, slept when she wanted and ate when she wanted. But most of all the house was quiet, and Rebecca liked quiet.

Jack liked noise. He liked loud sports, speedboats and motorcycles. Rebecca liked reading, and she would rather go sailing or bicycle riding. Jack liked the TV loud, he liked to talk on the phone loud and he liked to be around crowds of people in bars, sporting events and rock concerts. Rebecca did like to turn up her hip hop dance music while cleaning the house or working out, but for the most part, she would rather go to a museum or gallery or spend time at a library or coffee shop. Jack was an extrovert who liked to keep busy and have fun, while Rebecca was an introvert who liked to spend time alone.

Jack switched gears easily when he was around Rebecca, and Rebecca switched gears when she was working. Rebecca was a go-getter and she loved the challenge of her work. She had recently started her own PR firm, and she took pride in getting her clients the recognition they deserved. Because of Jack's support, Rebecca was able to be extremely picky about who she represented.

Jack kissed her again, on the lips this time slowly, tenderly. "I'll miss you, too."

Rebecca knew he meant it, because he always missed her. He really loved her. No one had ever loved her like Jack did, finally making her understand why people wanted to find love, be in love. She couldn't believe how much her life had changed. "You smell great," she murmured as she leaned in closer to his warm neck.

On the way to the kitchen, Rebecca grabbed Jack's suitcase and headed for the garage.

"Wait, Reb, I got it."

"I got it," Rebecca teasingly snapped back, suggesting she was perfectly capable of carrying a suitcase.

"You're so stubborn," he said and tried to grab it from her.

"Yes, I know."

He quickly got in front of her and opened his hatch. Before he had a chance to take the suitcase from her, she had already hoisted it up into the back of Jack's white Porsche Cayenne.

"Thank you," he said, playfully patting her bottom.

"You're welcome." Rebecca had always taken care of herself, which was one of the reasons Jack fell for her. And one of the reasons she drove him crazy. Jack was so good to her, and she felt she didn't do much for him in return. If she could carry his suitcase for him, fix a leaking toilet or put oil in his car, she was happy to do it. Plus, she recently learned that if you don't use your strength, you'll lose it. She remembered going out of town on a business trip herself and struggling to lift her computer bag up into the overhead compartment. That bothered her so much she started working out and lifting weights again. She loved feeling strong. But she had become a little lazy and comfortable after she and Jack were married.

It was gray and rainy on the hour and forty-five minute drive to the airport in Billings, and Rebecca was quiet.

"So you have a lot to do this week?" Jack asked.

"I do. My goal this week is to organize my office, clean out my files and become as paperless as possible. And I have to get more familiar with my new client Angie."

"Who is Angie? What does she do?"

"She's a writer and an advocate for women and children. She is doing incredible things. In fact, she sent me a packet full of what she is working on, her goals … I can't wait to dig in."

"Sounds like you'll be busy." He reached over and took her hand.

"You know, it's crazy. I thought this move to the country would ruin my career, but instead I love having a home office and the space. I have everything I need: computer, Internet, fax and phone."

"Oh, that reminds me, be careful when you take Lily for her walks. I saw another coyote close to the house."

"How close?"

"Next to the trees off the kitchen deck."

"That's close."

"Reb, you know the coyotes won't hurt you, but just make sure Lily doesn't get away from you. There's been too many lost cats and dogs in the area."

"Yeah, I know, it's awful. Don't worry. I won't let anything happen to our baby Lily." She lifted his hand and kissed it.

He pulled her hand to him and kissed hers back.

His phone rang, and he dropped her hand to answer it. Her hand rested on his thigh, and he tapped it as if to say I'm sorry. "Hello."

Rebecca noticed that her hand immediately went into its nervous position, her thumb nesting between her index and middle finger, which reminded her of the joke adults used to play on children about taking off their nose or removing their other thumb. Trying to distract herself from Jack's loud voice, she noticed her other hand was in the most nervous position—her thumb was between the middle finger and ring finger. She knew why; she most definitely knew why.

***

Rebecca remembered the night she was attacked by Roy Smythson. She was in Cheyenne at a friend's house planning to spend the night, but she became overwhelmed with the feeling she needed to go home. So she drove the hour drive back to Fort Collins, unsure of what was pulling her.

Rebecca unlocked the front door of her upstairs apartment, her keys jingling. Her cat Buddy was not meowing on the other side, awaiting her entrance as she normally did. It struck her as odd, but she continued inside. Buddy walked from her bedroom followed by Roy Smythson.

Shocked, Rebecca asked, "What are you doing here?"

Roy was somebody Rebecca had dated, but she hadn't seen him for several months.

"Hi, how are you? I thought I'd surprise you," he said, reaching out to give her a hug.

Rebecca put her hand up to stop him. "Give me my key!" she demanded. Suddenly it all made sense, the days she would come home from work and find things not quite the way she remembered leaving them. She'd thought she was going crazy.

"I don't have a key. The door wasn't locked. Here, check my pockets." He stuck his hands in his Dockers pockets and pulled the insides out. "I don't have a key. The door was open," he said, trying to sound convincing.

"The door was locked. I remember locking it."

"Well, I saw your landlord up here; maybe he forgot to lock it."

Rebecca wasn't going to let him talk his way out of it. He let himself into her apartment and back into her life uninvited. "Give me my key!" Rebecca said sternly, hiding her anxiety as she put her hand out again.

"Rebecca, I love you. Can we talk about this? I've really missed you. I want to work it out. Please, can I stay? Can we talk?"

"Where is my key?"

Roy grabbed Rebecca's hand and led her to the couch. "Rebecca," he said, starting to cry. "I want to tell you the truth because I want to make this work ..." He took a deep breath. "Your key is downstairs in your mailbox. I took the extra key out of your desk drawer a long time ago." He reached out to her with his crying eyes begging her to comfort him.

Rebecca refused.

"Rebecca, I want to come clean for us. This is really hard for me ..." He breathed another ragged breath. "I followed you to work every day. I stayed at your place all day while you were working. I've been reading your journal." He looked up at her. "I thought you were staying at your friend's house tonight? You wrote that you were staying with your friend." He paused then continued. "I've been through your garbage." He put his head down. "I'm sorry. I'm so sorry," he sobbed, his tears pleading for sympathy.

Rebecca gave him none.

"It hurts me so bad, what you write in your journal about me. Are you really happy to have me out of your life? Am I really that bad? Can't we work this out?"

Although Roy had made Rebecca nervous during the time they spent together, he was really scaring her now. There was nothing to save, in Rebecca's opinion. They never had been in a relationship; they had only dated. And his oblivion to what he was doing and had been doing to her terrified her. Roy was stalking her.

Keeping her anger and terror hidden, Rebecca said, "Why don't we start by you going downstairs and getting my key."

He stood up and happily dried his tears. Prancing, he left her apartment in stocking feet and without his coat. She hurried to the door and locked it—this was her first mistake and panic kept her from fixing it. She was supposed to make the 9-1-1 call first, then go to the door and hold it locked until the police came. It was February and very cold outside. So Roy would be less likely to run without his coat and shoes. He would be arrested by the police and she would be safe. Fear froze her as she stared at the phone across the room. Roy was out of her apartment and she was in control of the lock, but she was scared.

She could hear him coming back with her key.

Her fragile sense of control quickly shattered when he was there on the other side of the door, key in hole, trying and succeeding in turning it. He was begging, then demanding to be let in. Rebecca tried with all her might to hold the deadbolt locked, but she couldn't. She hoped his key would break, but the lock broke and her door flew open, pushing her back. She dropped into the fetal position to protect herself. He slammed the door, grabbed her hair and arm and dragged her kicking and screaming into the bedroom. He threw her onto the bed, straddled her and held her down.

Rebecca knew he would rape her. She was in shock.

"Did you call the police?" he hollered.

She didn't answer.

He hit her across the left side of her head, and suddenly, she could only hear a sharp buzzing in her left ear. Her head was throbbing. Everything became an echoing, red blur. She cried, begging him to stop. She tried to cover her face and ear before the next blow, but her arms were pinned beneath his legs.

"Did you call the police?"

Again, Rebecca didn't answer. If she answered yes, she feared she was in for a brutal beating or worse. If she answered no, she was in for a long night of torture. He punched her again and again.

But the physical pain couldn't compare to the humiliation and degradation she felt for allowing another human being to treat her this way.

He yelled once more, "Did you call the police?"

That time Rebecca heard herself cry, "No," through her tears, dreading that she'd given up the fight.

He jumped off her and ripped the bedroom phone cord from the wall, then rushed to the living room and yanked that phone cord, too.

Knowing this was her chance, Rebecca ran out of the apartment, out of the building and onto the stairs in the alley, screaming hysterically, "Help me! Help me! Call 9-1-1!" She clumsily hurried down the stairs holding tightly onto the railing. She feared he would kick her down the rest of the way. She turned to see if he was behind her as she hunched into a squat. She noticed her neighbor from across the hall looking out his window. She yelled to him, "Call 9-1-1!"

Roy stood at the top of the stairs, his face full of hate and anger. Holding his coat and shoes, he quickly turned and walked down the hall in the other direction.

Rebecca cautiously walked back to her apartment. She pulled his key from the lock and ran inside, leaving the door open. Her living-room phone was ruined so she rushed to her bedroom phone, all the while watching the door. Shaking, she plugged the line of her cordless phone back into the wall and finally made the call, 9-1-1.

Crying in dismay and shame, she stayed on the phone until the police arrived. Rebecca pressed charges. One officer left to look for Roy, the other took the report, while the third took pictures of her broken lock, the black marks on her hardwood floor from her shoes where Roy dragged her and the clump of her hair that was on her pillow where he held her down. He took pictures of her swollen and already bruising face, ear and arms.

The officer who took the report drove her to the hospital and brought her home when she was finished, four hours later. He went inside her apartment with her to make sure Roy wasn't there. He tried to persuade her to stay someplace else, but she refused. After looking around her place, the cop said he would keep an eye on the area and left.

When Rebecca was alone, she heard Buddy crying. During the attack, Buddy had forced herself under the stove, so Rebecca had to coax her out, and then she held Buddy's trembling body against her trembling body. The effect on Buddy made Rebecca thankful that she was her cat and not her child.

Rebecca locked her broken lock the best she could. She stuck a butter knife in the molding for added support and put a chair in front of the door. Rebecca slept on the couch cradling the phone, afraid, humiliated and exhausted.

***

That was the last time she saw Roy Smythson, she thought, as she heard Jack getting off his phone.

Jack took her hand again.

"I'll miss you," Rebecca said.

"If you say that again, I'm going to start believing you."

"I'll miss you." She leaned over and kissed him on the cheek. "I really love you."

He smiled. "What would you like to do next year for our anniversary? I have a few ideas, and I thought I should start planning now. But I'd like to hear what you would like to do before I book anything."

"Can I think about it and let you know when you get back?"

"Of course. I'm thinking Argentina, Greece or …"

"I've always wanted to see Greece."

"How about if you get a chance, see what you can find on the Internet, and we'll talk about it when I get back," Jack said. "You know, I've been thinking about buying a yacht, and I thought maybe we could lease one for two weeks to see if we like it. We could tour some of the islands in the Caribbean."

"That sounds wonderful." Rebecca started laughing.

"What?"

"I'm just picturing both of us sick hanging over the rail throwing up in the ocean."

Jack started laughing. "Could happen. Remember us deep sea fishing?"

"Yes, that's why it's a good idea to lease before we buy. We might hate it." Rebecca was still giggling.

"That deep sea fishing boat was small and the diesel smell was awful. I'm hoping to lease a ninety-two foot or bigger with three or more crew. I've made a few calls. It should run about forty to forty-five a week plus dockage, fuel and food." Jack started laughing. "We were both green, remember?"

"How could I forget! I was so glad to be back on land after that experience."

Jack's phone rang again, and Rebecca's mind drifted back to memories of Roy.

***

Roy ran.

For just over one year, she heard nothing about him or his case. She only knew that there was a warrant for his arrest and she was scared every day. She feared he was watching her.

Then Rebecca remembered coming home from work to find a white business envelope in her mailbox. She opened it as she climbed the stairs to her apartment. When she read State versus Roy Smythson, a wave of memories flooded over her and fear returned. She walked into her apartment and remembered everything as if it had happened just a few hours before. As her mind replayed the horror of that night, she began to cry. She didn't want to go through it all again. She had moved, and moved on with her life. Time had passed. The pain had gone and most of her hearing had returned. Rebecca had put that night behind her. She didn't want to go to court. She didn't want to see Roy.

A simple piece of paper with State versus Roy Smythson was rewinding her life to a place she didn't want to be. Though that night would never be forgotten, it had been dealt with and gently put behind her. Roy had already had two hearings. His next would be November thirteenth, Friday the thirteenth. If he pled not guilty, Rebecca would be dragged into court, not unlike being dragged into her bedroom on that horrible night so many months ago.

But before Rebecca could decide what to do, she had to return to the scene of the crime. She had to listen to her 9-1-1 call to remind her of what Roy had done to her soul. Seated in the Fort Collins courthouse in a private room with a tape recorder, she pressed play. What she heard horrified her. She sounded weak, wounded and beaten down. She sounded like a scared child, not a strong woman.

She vowed she would never be that person again.

That was when Rebecca knew she had to face this and follow it through to the end. She went to court on Friday the thirteenth. His lawyer was there, but Roy was a no-show. They issued another warrant, and Rebecca plunged back into her state of fear, not knowing if Roy would stalk her again or hurt her.

Initially, Rebecca stayed very involved with the case. She wanted to fight for her rights and, in doing so, fight for the rights of all women and victims. She wanted to do the right thing and leave her mark along the way, not the dragging marks on the floor from a victim, but strong marks in the law for other women.

But by the time the law caught up with Roy again, Rebecca was out of the loop. Too much time had passed, and Rebecca had changed. She had a future she was excited about that didn't include dredging up her past. She didn't go back to court and didn't hear another word about Roy—until she and Jack were in New York a month ago.

Jack and Rebecca were staying in a suite at the Four Seasons in Manhattan. Jack was there on business and Rebecca went along to visit her mother and meet with some clients and potential media contacts. The day before they headed home, Rebecca was in the bathroom when her cell phone rang. She was dancing around to hip-hop on the radio and drying off when Jack told her, "Somebody called you while you were in the shower."

"Who was it?"

"I don't know. I didn't answer it."

"It was probably my mom," she said as she started putting on her makeup.

"It's nice of her to take us out for lunch. What time will she be here?"

"Around noon." Rebecca headed to the living room to check her phone and Jack jumped into the shower. There was a message from a number she didn't recognize. She listened to the message, then slowly set the phone down on the table. Rebecca was stunned. She called the number back and talked to the woman who left the message. After hanging up, Rebecca's mind raced but she didn't know what to do, so she stayed sitting on the couch.

Jack came out of the bedroom. "What's wrong?"

"Remember I told you about that guy, Roy? Well, I guess he'll be released from prison next month and they wanted to warn me."

"He went to prison? For how long?"

"Five years," Rebecca answered, dazed.

"Reb, did you tell me everything? That's a long time."

"Yes, I told you everything, but it was a long time ago. I hardly remember that night myself," Rebecca lied. And she didn't know if she had told Jack everything. Did she just tell him he stalked her, or did she tell him that he busted her eardrum and bruised her body, face and self-worth? Did she tell him that he said he loved her and wanted to be with her? Did she tell him she feared being raped by him? She didn't know.

"Five years is a long time."

"I guess while he was on the run, he committed an armed robbery." She shook her head in disbelief. "And remember he was on the run for a couple years. He probably got more time for that."

"No, Rebecca. That's not what I mean. He deserved ten years or more for what he did to you. I'm just thinking that five years is a long time to sit and plan revenge."

"Why would you say that to me?" Rebecca snapped angrily. "You think he's coming after me?"

"I'm just saying we have to be careful," Jack backpedaled. "I'm sure he has better things to do with his life now. He probably got counseling, and he'll have to check in with a parole officer, right? I'm sure there's nothing to worry about."

"You know, you are giving me mixed messages! I don't know what you're talking about!"

"I'm sorry." He took a deep breath. "I don't know what I'm talking about either. I've just never been mixed up in anything like this before. I don't know what to say or do. Should I get you a bodyguard? Should I put a trace on him?"

Rebecca closed her eyes and took a deep breath herself. "Okay. Sit down and listen to me." She patted the couch next to her.

Jack sat down.

"I am going to write the date of his release on my calendar. I will not worry about it or think about it until then. I want you to do the same. When we get to next month, we will pay attention for a while and if nothing strange happens, then it's fine. I'm sure I will get a call if he leaves town or skips out on seeing his parole officer. This happened such a long time ago, can we please leave it alone. I'll remind you about this in a month and then we can worry if we want to, okay? Deal?"

"Deal."

They shook hands, then Jack kissed hers. "I love you and I won't let anything happen to you," Jack said.

"I love you, too. I won't let anything happen to you either." She smiled, and they finished getting ready.

4:50 PM

ON HER WAY home from the Billings airport, she had to drive across the state line back into Wyoming. She drove the long, hilly country roads deep in thought. The mountains were barely visible because of the cloudy weather, and the trees were beginning to change colors. She drove past several pastures filled with horses and a donkey in the mix, the theory being that donkeys hated coyotes and would attack them.

Rebecca thought about the phone call from Victim Services. The woman had said that Roy would be released from prison in a month, a month that had been up a week and a half ago. Rebecca didn't want to bother Jack or make him worry. And she didn't like how he had reacted, so she decided to keep it to herself. It was her problem. The attack happened long before Jack came into her life. Even though she really didn't think she had anything to worry about, she knew it would be in the back of her mind for a few months.

Right after Rebecca's warning about Roy's upcoming release from prison, she kept seeing him everywhere. She saw his eyes on the man who made her a vanilla latte at Starbucks. She saw his walk on a man crossing the street in front of her car. She smelled his cologne, Polo, on somebody at the movie theater. She heard his voice from a telemarketer. Although much time had passed, the memory of him was crystal clear, not because she wanted to remember, but because she felt she had to remember. She was more afraid than she wanted to admit, even to herself.

Rebecca thought about her past with Roy and how it tied in with all of her clients. There was Melody, a public speaker who spoke out on domestic violence; Angie, a writer who covered all women's issues and violence against women and children; and Angie's friend, Christy, a photographer who was also moving in the direction of helping women. All of her clients had one thing in common: they were all about improving the lives of women and children. And Rebecca's PR direction had come about because of what she went through with Roy.

Rebecca loved representing only women who wanted to make a difference or educate society, and she worked hard for her clients. Though she felt she was doing her part, she wished she could do more.

Because of her work and knowing how hard it was for some women, Rebecca sometimes felt guilty about her life. Jack helped her realize that as long as she was financially secure, she was able to do more for women and children: she could offer her services for a very reasonable fee and continue to limit her clients to only those who wanted to help and inspire women. "If Oprah lost it all or gave it away, how could she continue helping the way she does?" he asked her.

Success and money had bought Rebecca many things, but most importantly, security and safety. She thought about Jack's offer of a body-guard, which she could have because she could afford it. Money bought her a home with a security system. Money bought her new and reliable cars that didn't break down on the highway. Money bought new tires when they were needed and a full tank of gas. Money was security. Money was safety.

Often it was said that women wanted money or men with money, but maybe deep down women just wanted to be safe.

Rebecca noticed a car coming up from behind approaching her very quickly. She slowed down, thinking it was a cop. The car tailed her. Because of the rain and overcast sky, she couldn't tell if it was an unmarked police car. She checked her speedometer; she was going just two miles over the limit. She looked back to the road in front of her and noticed the straight, flat road ahead. There were no cars coming; clearly he could pass her. She continued driving, but kept glancing in the side and rearview mirrors. The car stayed on her tail. If she were to hit the brakes, he would hit her for sure. She slowed down a little more and pulled over to the side hoping he would pass her. He didn't. "If you're a cop, pull me over! If you're not, pass me!"

Suddenly she felt frozen, paralyzed. "Oh, my God! Is it Roy?" she pushed on the gas and the turbo kicked in, the sudden acceleration pressing her body against the seat. She exceeded the speed limit rapidly, but she didn't care. She wanted to get away from that car. She looked in the mirror again and she could see the headlights receding. In fact, the distance between them expanded so quickly that it appeared he had come to a complete stop right on the highway. She watched the headlights fade.

When she approached her driveway, she looked for that car or anything out of the ordinary. With no cars in sight, she pulled onto her long driveway. A line of pine trees on the right guided her to her beautiful home. Once she was in the garage with the door closed, she started to laugh at her cowardice. "He is not coming after me; over seven years have passed since he attacked me. I'm sure he has better things to do ... more important things on his mind."

Rebecca saw her beautiful white Bentley Continental convertible sitting in the center of their almost empty six-car garage. Jack had surprised her with it on her last birthday. A Bentley had always been her dream car— the car she would dream about, but never own. The day Jack bought it for her was the day she realized they were rich. As Rebecca peeked inside the car to admire the tan interior, she still couldn't believe that it was her car. She started giggling when she thought about the first time Jack drove her car.

***

Rebecca had been driving the Bentley for about a week and had all the controls set for herself: the seat position, the heat and air conditioning, even the XM radio was on her favorite station. They were going to take a trip into Denver.

"You should let me drive."

"No, it's my car," she said.

"… because the traffic … I'll have a headache if you drive."

Rebecca started laughing. "Fine."

They got inside and when Jack shut the driver's door, the seat started to move forward. He yelled, "Stop it! Stop it!"

Rebecca laughed hysterically while watching the seat continue to move forward. He was getting closer and closer to the steering wheel.

"Help! Help me!" Jack acted like he was being attacked by the car.

Rebecca kept laughing, offering no help. "You wanted to drive."

***

Still laughing over the memory, Rebecca walked into the house and locked the door behind her, something she and Jack never did. Lily jumped up on her, wanting some loving. Rebecca happily squatted down and gave her some. Lily licked Rebecca's cheek, danced around in circles and then ran out of the kitchen into the living room to get a toy. Rebecca turned back to the door and set the alarm, another thing she and Jack rarely did. But Rebecca did use the security system at night when Jack was out of town.

It was Sunday evening. She had the place to herself. She set her bag down on the counter, walked to the wine cellar and picked out a nice bottle of Chardonnay, then chose her favorite glass and set them both down on the counter. Next, she went downstairs to double check all the doors and windows, beginning in their gym. The doors were locked, with each door lock in the horizontal position. She checked the window locks as she walked the perimeter of the house, making sure they were in the lower, locked position.

Just after Rebecca and Jack returned from New York, Jack had hired a man to come over and check all of the door locks and windows. He tightened a few door knobs, checked all the windows and said everything looked secure. Jack had tried to act like it was just routine maintenance, but Rebecca knew it was because of Roy. Though Jack always appeared to be confident that Roy would not come back for her, he did little things to ensure their safety. His actions only scared her more because she doubted his confidence.

Rebecca stepped into the bar area where the pool table, dart board and video games waited to be played and checked the door; it was locked. She walked into the family room, and she checked that door as well. As Rebecca checked each door and window, she wondered if Roy would be able to find her if he wanted to. She had moved three times, and she was now married. She also wondered if taking Jack's last name would have made her safer.

Rebecca walked back upstairs to the main floor. With each step she took on the curved, dark oak stairway, her fear mounted. The open stairwell from the third floor all the way down to the first showed off the solid planks of wood hanging in the air. When they first got Lily, Rebecca was afraid that she would fall through the stairs. She still worried, but the stairway was beautiful.

When she and Jack first bought the house, they replaced all the carpeting with deeper, softer carpet. After the housekeeper would leave, Rebecca would run downstairs and make an angel on the freshly vacuumed floor. She'd move her arms and legs as if pushing snow to create the angel. Then she'd carefully get up and jump away from the angel to avoid making footprints in the carpet. She'd run upstairs to the third floor and look all the way down to the first floor where her angel lay. After she told her Dad how she made carpet angels, she received a Christmas card from him that read, "To the best little angel maker." She kept the card.

When Rebecca reached the main floor, she checked the spare bedroom with its doors that led out to a large deck. She hurried into her office to check that door and the windows in the other spare bedrooms. All the doors and windows were locked. Next, she went through the kitchen to double check the garage door and the doors off the breakfast nook that led out to an even larger deck overlooking the mountains. Those, too, were locked.

She returned to her office and wrote a quick note to herself, "Alarm," and taped it to the front door. That was the door she used to take Lily outside, and she didn't want to forget and set off the alarm herself. There were only two alarm controls, one by the garage door and one in their master bedroom. She wondered why there wasn't an alarm pad by the front door.

Finally, she checked upstairs: the master bedroom with its separate deck and double doors. Now she felt safe. She was locked in and everybody else was locked out. She changed into sweats and a tank top, then headed back downstairs. As Rebecca walked down the stairs she noticed a few things out of place, and she wanted everything neat and organized during this four days alone. She knew she wouldn't be able to concentrate on work if the house wasn't in perfect order. Starting in the kitchen, she quickly wiped down the counters after putting their morning coffee cups in the dishwasher. She also threw a load of towels into the washing machine. She skipped over the three spare bedrooms each with its own bathroom. Those doors remained closed so Lily wouldn't go in and knock the pillows off the beds. Rebecca always told Lily that she got that trait from her father, because Jack didn't like throw pillows either. Rebecca and Jack spent many nights laughing as Lily would walk up and down the length of their large sectional in the living room knocking every loose pillow off the couch onto the floor.

Because Jack and Rebecca were tidy people and they had a house-keeper who came every Friday, there really wasn't much for Rebecca to do. But walking through the house, making sure everything was in order, made her feel better. The only two messy rooms in the house were their offices, and she was fine with that because they always were. But Rebecca's office wouldn't be a mess for long.

Rebecca fed Lily, then took her outside to pee. She was so happy she had Lily in her life, but hated admitting that she got her from a pet store at the mall.

***

One day not long after her cat Buddy passed away, Rebecca was at the pet store in the mall looking at the cat toys and thinking about Buddy when she noticed a cute little pug behind the glass. She asked the store clerk if she could see the pug. Rebecca played with Lily for about twenty minutes, then handed her back to the clerk and left the store. The next day, Rebecca went back into town again to see if the pug was still there. She was, so Rebecca played with her again then left the store again. The following day and third time in the store, she realized she couldn't bear the thought of anybody else owning her. She had to have that dog. So Rebecca filled out the paperwork, paid twelve hundred dollars and took Lily home with her.

Rebecca and Lily went to Pet Smart, and Rebecca bought everything she could possibly need for her new baby. She had only had Buddy before so having a dog was a whole new experience. She bought books and magazines about pugs and dog training.

She was a little nervous about buying Lily while Jack was out of town, but when he came home, he was thrilled. He loved little Lily from the start.

"She's ours?" Jack asked.

"Yes," she said and handed her to Jack.

"Does she have a name?"

"I hope you're okay with Lily."

"Baby Lily." He kissed Lily's head. "She's so little … and cute."

"I know. She's naughty too. She pees a lot."

"So we're potty training now."

"Yes, let me tell you what I've learned." She led them to the couch to sit down, urging him to keep holding Lily or she would pee. She explained crate training. Lily needed to sleep in her crate so she would learn to hold her potty until morning. Rebecca also had a long baby gate to keep her in the kitchen nook with the hardwood floors. Agreeing with everything Rebecca explained to him, Jack also read the books to better understand their new baby.

A month later when Rebecca went out of town on business, she trusted Jack to be consistent with Lily. Two days later she came home about ten o'clock at night and found Jack cuddling Lily in bed, both of them fast asleep. She smiled, leaned over and kissed them.

Lily never slept in her crate again, and the spoiling had begun.

6:20 PM

REBECCA HIT POWER on the stereo and turned toward the kitchen. She was suddenly struck with fear, ducking in panic. She quickly turned back and turned the volume dial to off. She stood there for a second shaking from that sudden shock of blaring music. "Nice, Jack!" she said in disgust. She turned the volume down and tuned the satellite radio to Lite Jazz. The jolt of blaring music alone could have put her in a bad mood, but she wasn't going to let it. The jazz was soothing, and she started to relax again.

Rebecca headed to the kitchen and poured herself a glass of wine. She grabbed the large folder she had received in the mail from Angie, turned on the fireplace using the remote control, and made herself comfortable on the chaise lounge in the living room. Lily jumped up and lay down next to her. Rebecca glanced at the clock; it was six-thirty and starting to get dark outside. She turned on the lamp next to her.

"What do we have here?" Rebecca pulled everything out and started going through Angie's things. There was a note from Angie.

Hi Rebecca,

I know you said you wanted to learn more about me and what I'm doing, so I put this together for you. I've worked with the National Coalition for the Protection of Children and Families. I've also been very involved in community education and the Community Notification Act. I've worked with Morality in Media, women's prisons, and I've been a guest speaker for convicted male sex offenders and Take Back the Night. I've written several articles for local and national magazines and newspapers (included in packet) and there have been several articles written about me. I think there's even a novel based on my life called The Gentlemen's Club. I've just started reading it, and I love it.

Please call me if you have any questions or need more information on any of these topics.

Angie
P.S. I'm looking forward to working with you!

The first thing Rebecca read was the transcript of a speech Angie had given to six hundred Boston high school students while she was working on a domestic violence case just outside Boston.

During her talk, a bell chimed every fifteen seconds representing a woman who had just been abused in the United States.

Angie introduced herself as a public speaker, writer and part owner of a national women's newspaper. She said she used her medium to write and speak out against violence against women and children.

Angie explained violence to the kids. "Violence against women, teenagers and children is very much intertwined and connected. Violence is sexual abuse, physical abuse, stalking, fearing physical abuse and witnessing abuse in the home. Violence is rape, sexual assault and all forms of prostitution, including strip clubs and pornography. Violence is when children are kicked out of the home or feel the need to leave to get away from violence. And there is a direct link between child sexual abuse, rape, prostitution, depression, addictions, domestic abuse, pornography and runaways. Statistics show that anybody who goes through some form of violence or abuse and doesn't get help is more likely to end up going through more abuse, such as an abusive marriage, rape, other forms of abuse or abusing others, homelessness, drug or alcohol addiction, eating disorders, suicide and prostitution."

Angie asked the students to think about their lives while she shared her own story. Her father left the family when she was an infant, leaving her feeling unloved and abandoned. She was molested at age eleven by a friend of the family; she felt alone, embarrassed, humiliated, guilty and different from others. She married young and found herself the victim of domestic abuse; she felt fearful, alone and confused. She ran to save her life and eventually found herself homeless and contemplating becoming a prostitute as a stripper. She felt desperate, useless, and was in emotional pain.

Rebecca took a sip of wine. She had felt all of that after being attacked by Roy.

Angie explained the cycle of abuse, the signs of a potential abuser and self-esteem issues. She talked about how her life was a perfect example of what happens to a victim of abuse who doesn't get help: abuse leads to lower self-esteem, which in turn leads to self-destructive behavior and self-inflicted abuse.

Angie's way of getting her life back on track consisted of reaching out for help, getting counseling and finding a place to live. She found someone to help her with her finances, and she decided to go back to school. Angie regained her self-respect, her morals and her values. She had to find direction in her life; she had to have goals and dreams, so she could have a bright future. She chose writing.

Angie talked about how hard it was to take her life back and what it felt like to start moving in the right direction. After each positive incident in her life, she felt stronger, more hopeful, and more honorable. She finally had control of her life and her future. She believed in and respected herself.

Rebecca thought about her own experience when she was too afraid and weak not to call the police for help. They referred her to Victim Services. She was thankful that she started getting counseling and the help she needed right away. She was thankful that she realized she needed that help.

Rebecca choked up because she could also relate to those feelings of pride and strength. She was a little surprised by the similarities between Angie and her. She didn't realize how experiences weren't as important as the feelings the experiences created when connecting with other women.

Angie wrapped up her talk by sharing her joys and successes, answering questions and recapping the importance of reaching out for help, guarding your values and morals and going for your dreams and goals. She also gave each of the students a handout filled with hotline telephone numbers to call if they needed help.

Several newspaper clippings were attached to the transcript of Angie's speech with interviews about her talk. Clearly, Angie attracted the media, which would make Rebecca's job that much easier.

Rebecca wrote a few notes about violence against women and children, then got up and went to the kitchen. The wind was picking up and, as solid as it was, the house groaned and rattled a little in the strong gusts, startling her from time to time. She poured another glass of wine and went back to the living room.

She wondered why, after being attacked by Roy, she couldn't get to the phone fast enough, but when Angie was sexually abused and abused by her husband, she didn't tell anybody.

Rebecca wrote, "Was it the age of the victim, the type of violence or both? Are children easier to manipulate? Are women groomed into accepting violence? Had Angie been taught to accept violence?"

Rebecca stood in the living room and looked out the wall of windows. She watched the wind race through the trees. Though it was almost dark, she searched for coyotes and strange cars but saw nothing out of the ordinary. Then she thought about Roy and how they met.

***

Rebecca was the assistant to Ed, a writer and editor for the local newspaper. Roy had been Ed's childhood friend and had just moved back to town the last year. Roy had called often and wanted to put a face to the woman he kept talking to. From the start, Rebecca had a feeling he was trouble, but he was attractive and interested in her, and she was flattered. He asked her out the first time they met.

Rebecca had spent Saturday cleaning her apartment and pampering herself, getting ready for her first date with Roy. When she finished cleaning her place, she placed a pot of water on her stove burner to simmer. She added vanilla and lavender-scented potpourri to the water. Rebecca loved when her apartment smelled good. She didn't bake or cook so she learned to enjoy the scents of candles and potpourri. Some of her favorite scents were vanilla, sugar cookies, birthday cake, lavender and sometimes cinnamon.

Roy seemed nice and had a great job as a firefighter. There was an allure to dating a rescuer. In most people's eyes, firefighters were heroes. She secretly hoped that he would be the one. Rebecca knew she would like to settle down someday and why not with a superhero. Rebecca hadn't been on a date for a while, and she was excited.

When Roy came to the door to pick her up, he looked amazing. His dark hair, bright blue eyes and tan skin added up to a very good-looking man. And he smelled great; she had always liked Polo.

"Are you ready?" he asked.

"Yes, I'm all set." She grabbed her keys and bag, locked the door behind her and followed him down the stairs to his truck. He opened the door for her, and she got in. He waited until she was settled in, then closed the door behind her.

They had already decided on Chinese, and they were both quiet on the way to the restaurant. He was shy, which she didn't expect because Ed had made him out to be so much fun, outgoing, life of the party.

He seemed nervous until their food arrived. Roy and Rebecca talked and ate, both relaxing as the time passed.

About halfway through their meal Rebecca panicked. "I have to go!" she demanded. "I have to go home right now!"

"Why? Are you okay?"

"Yes, but I have to go home!"

"Okay. I'll get some take-home containers." He turned to look for their server.

"Okay."

"Did I say something that offended you?"

"No," she said, "but I can't tell you."

"Why can't you tell me what happened?"

"Because you're a firefighter."

"What?"

"Roy! I left my stove on at home!"

She could tell he was trying not to laugh. "I'm sure it will be okay."

"I don't think so. If the water dries up, the potpourri will start on fire!"

The server came over.

"We need take-home boxes and the bill, because we have an emergency at home."

Rebecca liked how he made it sound like they had a home together.

"I'll be right back," the server said.

Rebecca's stomach was aching. Things were not moving quickly enough. She kept picturing her place on fire. She couldn't focus on anything except getting home. And Buddy was in her apartment.

Rebecca was antsy on the drive home and couldn't understand Roy's calmness. His lack of concern angered her. It was as if he didn't care because it wasn't his house burning down. He let people cut in front of him; he didn't run yellow lights. It wouldn't be all of his things ruined, she thought as she worried about her neighbors and the others in the building. What if she caused the fire that would destroy people's lives or kill people who lived in the building?

When they got to her apartment, Rebecca ran up the stairs and into her apartment, which smelled strongly of lavender. Roy followed at his own pace. She ran into the kitchen and saw there was still water in the pot. Everything was fine. She turned the burner off and walked back into the living room where Roy was bent over petting Buddy.

"Is everything okay?"

"Yes, it's fine. But I'm exhausted." She put her hand on her forehead for a moment, then pushed her hair back. Her energy had been sucked away by her panic and his unwillingness to share her urgency.

"Oh, yeah. I understand. Let me go and get your food. I'll be right back."

Rebecca calmed down and feared she had given him the wrong idea; she was still interested. She just thought their date started off badly and it was her fault. She decided to ask him if he wanted to stay and finish eating. He didn't, but they did continue seeing each other.

After only a couple of dates, he considered Rebecca his girlfriend and started showing his true colors. He called her at all hours of the night to either share an exciting story or idea he had or to complain about problems at work, or with family or friends. He seemed to have a lot of problems with life in general. Nothing was ever his fault. Most of their conversations consisted of her trying to "fix" him and all of his troubles. Roy's odd behavior, full of energetic highs and devastating lows, concerned Rebecca enough that she did research on the computer and diagnosed Roy as being bipolar. It was the only thing that made sense. His moods were hard to keep up with.

On good days, Roy was fun to be around. He was energetic and made her laugh. A couple of their dates were so good that she found herself thinking about a future with him. But on their bad dates, he hardly talked to her or anybody. He seemed to hate life and everybody in it.

***

Rebecca kissed Lily's soft jowls and backed away to look at her. She noticed how every time Lily exhaled a breath, her cheeks would expand like she was playing the tuba. Rebecca started laughing, then kissed her again; Lily's tail started to wag.

Rebecca read more of Angie's work and learned more about the horrifying abuse at strip clubs. Besides the derogatory name calling and the grabbing of their breasts and buttocks, these women said that men attempted and often succeeded in penetrating them with their fingers. Their customers also exposed their penises, rubbed their penises on them and masturbated in front of them. The young women were propositioned for prostitution daily.

Rebecca was continually astounded about the strip club facts and statistics. She didn't understand why this was going on, how women could do this for a living and why they rationalized that it was okay to be treated that way. She feared men who treated women in such a way, women who were daughters, sisters, nieces and oftentimes mothers.

Rebecca thought about co-workers who would go to strip clubs with their husbands or boyfriends or even with a group of girlfriends. She could never understand those women, but she always figured that if women were going to strip clubs, their presence would keep men in check. She wanted to believe that the men would be less likely to try to finger the dancers or take their penises out in front of the other "normal" women. She thought the strippers were a little safer when there were female customers in the clubs. Rebecca wondered if the female spectators realized the gritty truth of degradation and violence against women in the strip clubs.

Several years ago, Rebecca remembered flipping through the channels on TV and stopping on Howard Stern interviewing a stripper. He asked the stripper if she had been sexually abused as a child. She said that she had been. There was such sadness in her eyes. He said every stripper he had ever talked to had been molested when they were little. Rebecca couldn't believe that Howard Stern knew the horrific statistics about the industry. Unfortunately, it didn't stop him from asking her to get naked and crawl under his desk. And so she did.

After reading through more of Angie's papers, Rebecca couldn't understand why Angie didn't exploit the one thing that made her special. She didn't share it with the kids in Boston, and she didn't include any articles in the packet about her being shot at the strip club. Rebecca, however, knew all about it, because she always researched new clients.

After writing a few more notes, Rebecca headed to the kitchen to get another glass of wine. Lily stayed on the chaise lounge, snoring loudly. Rebecca giggled to herself, "Not a watch dog, that's for sure."

When Rebecca walked back into the living room, she noticed that the fire was starting to heat up the house. A good time to take Lily outside, she thought, and the warm house would feel good when they came back inside. She went back into the kitchen to turn off the alarm.

"Lily, you wanna go outside?" Lily perked up so quickly her ear landed on top of her head, and Rebecca laughed out loud about her crazy clown Lily. "I sure love you, Lily baby. Let's go outside."

Almost immediately, the coyotes started yipping back and forth, echoing though the hills. Lily barked back into the darkness. She barked straight up toward the hill, then suddenly turned and barked behind her toward the driveway. Rebecca was scared and didn't like Lily's reactions, so she decided to go back inside. "Come on Lily. We'll try again later." Rebecca closed and locked the door behind them. She unhooked Lily, slipped off her shoes and headed straight to the alarm system to rearm it, noticing that the red light was illuminated when the alarm was set. She shivered in the warm house but not from being cold. She hated taking Lily out at night, especially when Jack was out of town.

Rebecca sat back down on the chaise with Lily and took a sip of her wine. Still faintly hearing the coyotes outside, she reached for the remote and turned the jazz a little louder to drown out their howling. Rebecca pet Lily's side, touching the scar on her hip from a coyote attack and that horrifying morning came flashing back.

***

Rebecca woke suddenly to Jack's yelling. Rebecca sprung out of bed and heard the front door slam. She knew in an instant Lily had been attacked by a coyote. She looked out the window and saw two coyotes running from the yard to the woods with Jack behind them yelling. Rebecca started to cry. She couldn't see Lily. Jack turned and looked up at the window. He saw Rebecca, then bent over to call Lily.

"Please Lily ... Please be okay."

She saw Lily walk up to Jack, wagging her tail. Jack looked back up to the window, guilt ridden. Rebecca ran down the hall and down the stairs to meet them at the front door. Lily was bleeding from the back of her neck, hip and rear of her left leg. She smelled horribly and was filthy, but she seemed to be okay. But Jack felt awful, Rebecca could tell.

Rebecca looked over Lily to see how badly she was hurt. The smell and dirt made it hard to tell the extent of her injuries, so Rebecca rushed her upstairs and into their big master tub. She ran lukewarm water and put Lily in, washing her with antibacterial soap and water. When she was finished Lily started bleeding worse, so Jack and Rebecca drove her to the animal emergency about forty-five minutes away. It was five-thirty in the morning.

On the drive over, Jack kept apologizing.

"Honey, it's not your fault. If anything you're our hero. You chased off those two coyotes," Rebecca said as she held Lily tighter. "Daddy's a hero, huh, baby? Daddy's our hero."

Jack reached over and pet Lily. "I'm sorry, baby."

"What's that?" Rebecca pretended that Lily had whispered something to her. "Oh. Okay, I'll tell him." She looked at Jack. "She's mad at you."

"I know. I'm sorry I put you out there."

"No, it's not that. She's mad at you because she has no neighborhood friends, and she meets two fun friends and Daddy chases them away."

"I won't laugh until I know she's okay."

"She'll be just fine, honey. I think we were very lucky. I keep remembering all the times she wanted out and I just tied her outside. I didn't watch her; I wouldn't have been able to hear her. That scares me so much, I'm sick about it."

"Yes, we've been lucky. I just had no idea they would come up to the house like that. Brazen. I hope she's okay."

They left the hospital loaded with horror stories about the local coyotes, medication for Lily, and Lily shaved in several areas with a staple in her hip. The vet said they were lucky; one second later and there would have been an entirely different outcome.

On the drive home, Jack said, "I tied her out like bait. I just can't believe it. Did you see them?"

Rebecca could tell he was fighting tears. "Yes, I saw them. I can't believe it either."

"Reb, I attached the cable to her harness. I turned and went inside the house. You know, she is right there by my office window."

Rebecca nodded.

"I sat down in my chair, heard a noise, looked out and started yelling. It happened that fast."

"They saw you put her there."

"They must have. They must be in the woods behind us watching the house, waiting for an opportunity."

"Don't scare me."

"Rebecca, we have to be careful. Lily can't be outside alone ever again."

"You're right. I'm still sick about how many times we have left her outside alone. I wonder why now, why this morning?"

"I guess it's the time of the year, fall moving in. And remember what the vet said, first thing in the morning and around dusk seem to be the most dangerous times for small animals, family cats and dogs."

Rebecca pet Lily lying on her lap. "Lily, we're not good parents."

"We'll get better. We're learning." He reached over and rested his hand on Lily's back. "Lily honey, I don't want you hanging around those friends anymore. Do you understand me? They're no good. They play too rough."

"I agree with your father. Those two are not allowed to play over here ever again." Rebecca held onto Jack's hand and kissed it. "Thank you for saving my baby's life." Tears welled up in her eyes.

Jack kissed Rebecca's hand back.

"What if they would have gone after you?"

"They wouldn't. They're afraid of humans."

"How do you know?"

"They ran off when I started yelling."

"I saw them, Jack. You were outside, and they were not that far from you. They didn't run off very fast. And what about that woman the vet told us about who had to play tug-of-war with her dog on a leash. That coyote wasn't afraid of her. I'm a lot smaller than you. Would they have gone after me? If they would come that close to the house and they didn't run off as quickly as I think they should have. I'm a little nervous."

"Honey, I really don't think you have to be afraid. The coyotes are hunting during dusk and dawn. I'm almost always home during those times, so I'll take her out then."

"No, I don't want to be afraid in my own yard. I like where we live. I'll just keep my eyes out and scream like a crazy person if I see one heading our way."

Lily snorted. Jack and Rebecca giggled.

***

The coyote howls grew louder and closer, jolting Rebecca back to the present. She knew that the coyotes were more active again because of the season. It was getting colder and the nights were longer, getting dark earlier in the evening and staying dark later in the morning. Rebecca gave Lily a kiss on the head. "We were so lucky, baby."

7:50 PM

THE PHONE RANG, and Rebecca jumped.

"Honey, it's Dad. I've been watching the news, and I just wanted to tell you about some recent coyote attacks where people are being attacked. Those coyotes are getting less fearful of humans."

"Are you serious? Where? Who?"

"Here in Colorado and I think Kansas. Oh, and a young woman was killed in Canada. You may want to do a little research of your own to find out more. But I thought about you and Lily, and I know Jack's away. I want you to be careful."

"I will, Dad. Thanks for calling."

"Yes, and do you know what to do if you see one and he isn't shying away from you?"

"Well, I guess Lily and I would run into the house."

"Becky, if you see one, don't turn your back on him."

Rebecca always felt like a child when he called her that. He was the only one who could get away with it.

"Make as much noise as you can and make yourself look big by raising your arms up. Maybe you should pick up Lily and hold her, but make a lot of noise. Even if one gets close to you and starts to circle you, don't turn your back on him, okay?"

"Okay, Dad, but you're scaring me."

"Well, Becky, I want you to know what to do. You're out there living with the coyotes. I wish you and Jack would consider getting a gun."

"Dad, we're not getting a gun. We've had this talk. I don't want a gun in this house."

"… well maybe I should come and stay with you, at least while Jack's out of town. This is a bad time of year; those coyotes are hungry."

Rebecca thought that it would be nice to have him around for a while, not because of the coyotes but because she missed him. He would also help ease her mind about Roy. But her dad didn't know anything about Roy, and she wanted to keep it that way. Plus, she needed time to herself to get her work done. "Dad, I'm fine. I have a ton of work to do and I'm staying safe. I honestly don't go far from the house. I've heard the coyotes, but I haven't seen any since Jack left. Lily and I will be fine. But thanks for the information. I will use it if I need to. I love you, Dad."

"I love you too, honey. You call me if you change your mind or if you need anything, okay?"

"Okay, I will." She hung up the phone.

***

Rebecca was raised by her father and grew up on the wrong side of the tracks. She lived in a tough neighborhood, went to the toughest schools, and had the toughest friends. Her friends were like her; some of them had hard home lives and not much money, but she always felt safe and happy and loved by her friends.

Because of her father and her friends, Rebecca didn't learn about the submissive role of a female. She didn't know that a girl couldn't beat up a boy if he deserved it; she didn't know that a girl couldn't be ready to throw down if she needed to. She liked being a little rough around the edges.

Although Rebecca felt tough and feisty at times, the last time she got together with her old neighborhood friends, she was reminded that she was usually the one in the background, watching.

"The follower," they teased, "not feared … or tough …"

"Oh, yeah," Rebecca laughed and flexed her muscles. "Did you have the nickname 'Rocky' when you were in junior high?"

They all rolled their eyes and laughed at her.

It was true and it suited her just fine. She had never been loud or a fight instigator; she was usually behind the others keeping quiet. But Rebecca did have her share of problems. She had been provoked into fights and had been sent to the principal's office a few times for doing things like ditching class to drive a sick friend home or starting a friendly food fight in the lunchroom. It was during that last visit with her friends Cecilia, Rachel, Vicki and Lupe that she realized they had taught each other to be strong. She felt honored to have such strong and loyal friends.

Rebecca knew her dad trusted her, though he rarely knew what she was doing. She had the feeling he knew that she could be a little impish, but he didn't know that she often stayed out all night and occasionally smoked and drank with other kids from the wrong side of town. He was disappointed in her at times, but never angry. Rebecca's dad had two rules for his girls: graduate from high school and don't have sex until after you graduate from high school. Rebecca was sure she could follow both rules, but she was never too sure about her older sister Lisa.

Rebecca's life revolved around her friends, fun and a little bit of trouble, while Lisa's life revolved around boys, makeup, bras and panties, high-heeled shoes and designer clothing that they never could afford. Lisa was in love with a new boy, heartbroken and fighting with a friend every other week. Lisa shared her life's dramas openly with their dad, whereas Rebecca kept everything to herself because she didn't think she had much worth sharing. Rebecca laughed remembering when she got her period and how all her friends got together to teach her how to use a tampon. She was the late bloomer of the group.

***

Rebecca would love to plan another get together with her old friends. Class reunions just never came often enough.

The phone rang again. It was Jack's mom calling to tell her that she had seen the same coyote special on TV. She said she believed that both of the attacks in the United States had been on children, and the Canadian woman had also been small.

Rebecca became even more afraid of the coyotes.

She thought about when Jack's parents and Rebecca's dad had helped them move into their country home. They claimed they came for moral support, but they really came to see the house. Jack's mom had fun bossing around the movers, which was fine with Rebecca. Their dads enjoyed looking over the utility room, hanging pictures and spending time outside in the country.

When they found what was left of a freshly killed porcupine, they became aware of the coyotes in the area. Then when Lily joined their family, Rebecca's dad was immediately uneasy. Jack and Rebecca wished that they had paid more attention to his concerns.

Rebecca leaned over and kissed Lily's head again, then reached for Angie's packet to pick up where she had left off. She pulled out a sheet of paper with disturbing photographs of women in pornography. Below the four photos of women in bondage were four photos of the prisoners from the Abu Ghraib prison scandal. The photos were the same: a woman being peed on and a prisoner being peed on; a woman lying on the cement floor tied up in bondage and blindfolded and a prisoner tied up and blindfolded in bondage; women naked in a pyramid and prisoners naked in a pyramid. Rebecca was disgusted, "I guess if you're a woman you are supposed to like this kind of treatment, but not if you are a prisoner of war."

Lily sat up quickly startled by the sound of Rebecca's voice. Rebecca pet Lily. "I'm sorry, honey. Mama's just talking out loud."

At the bottom of the sheet it said, "There was such outrage about the prisoners. Where is the outrage for what is happening to our daughters?"

"That is so true …" again Rebecca exclaimed, wondering how the women in pornography and prostitution felt after seeing the Iraqi prisoner photos. She wondered if they made the connection. Rebecca thought about the constitution and the first amendment. She was certain that the first amendment was never intended to protect people who wanted to hurt children and young women.

Next Rebecca read Angie's article, "Pornographic Material Needs Warning Label."

Pornographic material can be as destructive as cigarette smoking. The sale, distribution and use of it put everyone in danger, including men. This destructive pollution relies on men to make their industry billions of dollars. In exchange, the men are losing their families, becoming impotent and losing the sense of reality of women and how they want to be treated.

The same way cigarette advertisements go after children, pornography goes after men. They start with the bait: Women.

Some women who are forced and others who have such low self-worth feel their bodies are the only way to survive in this country. The same message is created by this industry. Then, they assure men it's okay to participate by backing it with false information about men and women concerning sex. Everything from soft-porn magazines to hard-core pornography is filled with these harmful messages, and men accept it and believe in it.

This industry encourages men to lie to their wives or stay single, knowing that a man's wife is less likely to put up with pornography in the home; therefore the enterprise loses a buyer and loses money. So while men are trying to convince women to "get with the times" or "I only have it for the articles," women must understand that men are being victimized, too.

An obsession with pornography isn't completely the man's fault. Not only does pornography cause a hormonal change, there is also a chemical reaction in the brain causing the inability to differentiate between reality and fantasy, and, in a lot of men, it's an addiction. It starts with a soft-core magazine that leads to an uncontrollable hunger where satisfying it becomes more and more difficult.

Like cigarettes, we need warning labels on all pornographic material. WARNING: Pornography may cause an illusional way of looking at women, children and sex. It may cause impotency and addiction. It can also lead to the destruction of your family or the inability to have one.

In addition, we need hot lines and support in every state to help men realize it's a problem before it's too late.

Rebecca liked the different angle in the article, that men were also victims of pornography. She loved the idea of a group of great, strong men getting together and suing the sex industry the way people sued the tobacco industry. They could argue they were never warned that looking at pornography could become an addiction, or cause a loss of money and time. They didn't know they could lose their families, lose their ability to have an erection without pornography or lose touch with reality when it came to women and children.

She thought about how laws were changed to protect nonsmokers so maybe laws could be made to protect women and children, especially considering that pedophiles and rapists often use pornography before committing violent crimes against women and children. Clearly, laws can be changed, amendments can be made.

Rebecca and Lily were worried by a sudden gust of wind that sounded like sand being thrown against the windows. It was raining again. The rising wind was like nothing Rebecca had experienced before and she was scared. Fearing the windows would come crashing in, she grabbed the remote and closed all the blinds to the big living-room windows. The blinds would at least block the glass from spilling into their home. Lily was also upset. Rebecca turned up the stereo and tried to relax.

She thought about that card she received from Roy that was still in her office: To: Rebecca, An Angel in my Heart. From: Roy. The memory of when she received the flowers and card made her smile. It wasn't all bad. She actually had a couple of great memories of Roy.

***

Rebecca had stayed home from work because she wasn't feeling well; she told her boss she would work from home. There was a knock on her door. When she opened the door, flowers and a white paper bag were sitting on the floor. She bent over to pick them up, and there was Roy with a surgical mask covering his face. "Is it safe to come it?"

Rebecca laughed. "Yes, it is." She held up the bag, "Chicken soup?"

"Chicken soup." He lowered his mask and followed her inside. Roy also had two movies so, needless to say, she didn't get any work done. But she did have a lot of fun with Roy. He stayed with her most of the day and never made a pass. He waited on her, teased her and let her nap.

It was ironic, but that was her favorite memory of him and probably the exact day he took the key to her apartment. She tried to remember. She knew she had fallen asleep during one of the movies, and she left him alone when she went to the bathroom. Roy had only been in her place two or three other times before he started stalking her.

Rebecca remembered the time they had gone out for lunch; he had a wandering eye, he was moody and inconsiderate. When they got to her place to watch a movie, she was annoyed and didn't want him there. Before they started the movie, he used her bathroom. She went in after him, closed the door and saw his footprints on her freshly cleaned rug. She could clearly see his footprints facing the toilet where he stood while peeing. With his footprints irritating her so much, she knew she had bigger issues with Roy, and she told him she wasn't feeling well and he had to go. After he left, she shook out her rug and knew she had to end it.

But Roy convinced her to go out with him one more time. So they went to a trendy restaurant, then for drinks to a bar with a band. They both knew a couple of guys in the band. The evening started off nicely, and she was glad she'd given Roy one more chance. But later in the night he seemed nervous and troubled, almost angry for no apparent reason, and Rebecca knew it would be their last date. She had had enough of her erratic dates with Roy. She told him she had to get going. He didn't want to go but agreed to take her home. On their walk to the car in the bar parking lot, Roy pulled out a single cigarette and started smoking. The shock of Roy smoking made her laugh. "I didn't know you smoked."

Roy didn't look like the smoking type, yet he seemed very comfortable with the cigarette between his fingers. "I don't smoke much. I bummed it from the guy at the door. And the matches."

Rebecca grabbed his arm and stopped him in the middle of the parking lot. "I can French inhale."

"No, you can't. You don't smoke."

"I know. But I can French inhale."

"Let's see." He handed her the lit cigarette.

As she took a puff, he stood in front of her, facing her. She figured it was to get a good look, but just as she started to push the smoke from her mouth and breathe it into her nose, Roy bent to kiss her. Rebecca started coughing like she always did while attempting her smoking stunt, so the kiss barely happened. She was glad she coughed. On the drive home, she wondered how she could avoid the goodnight kiss or even his attempts to come inside.

On the other hand, she thought about how nice it would be to get a little loving. She had a slight buzz and Roy smelled good and looked even better. It had been a while, and he was attractive, took care of himself, and had a touch of bad boy in him. She was sure the sex would be good. But her boss would know all about her sexually; it seemed Roy kept telling him stories about her. She couldn't imagine anything long term with Roy. Too messy, she decided.

Men seemed to think women were so lucky when it came to sex and men. It wasn't that simple, even though Rebecca wished it were. When she was younger, she sometimes wanted a one-night stand, but she always had to weigh the situation. Too many times she thought she was having a fling only later to discover she had unknowingly entered into a relationship. She had also had experiences where once a man had sex with her, he suddenly felt he owned her. Rebecca feared Roy would feel like that because they had already spent a fair amount of time together.

They sat in the car and talked briefly. Rebecca said she was tired and had to get up early. She also decided to flatter him so he wouldn't feel the need to walk her to the door. "Will you do me a big favor? Will you stay here and watch me until I get inside my apartment? It's late and dark."

"Let me walk you in."

"No, it's fine, but please stay until I get in. You'll see my light."

"Sure, no problem."

Handshake? No. Kiss on the check? No. Hug? No. So she did nothing but thanked him and got out of the car. She turned back, smiled and waved.

She was glad that they'd taken turns paying on their dates. Her dates with Roy had been strange—one date, she liked him; the next date, she didn't. It felt like she was dating twins: one nice and one evil. She would call him in a couple days and tell him it wasn't going to work out, but she would like to stay friends. She hated that she was afraid to tell him that she was not interested. She hated that she felt weak and strangely scared to tell him the truth.

About a week and a half after she told him that they were better off as friends, he moved into the apartment next to hers.

Rebecca started attending a women's group to help empower women and teach basic skills that women had forgotten or never learned, like boundaries, communication, definitions of abuse and how to set and achieve goals. The other women who attended the group had boyfriends or husbands who hated that they attended such a course. She figured the guys were fearful of losing the women they had trained so well, and she learned from these women that they wanted out but were afraid and didn't know how to get out.

One woman, Mary, said that her plan was to tell her boyfriend that she needed a break to re-evaluate the relationship and she needed him to stop coming over. She wasn't breaking things off entirely; maybe they could date and see how it went. Of course, this was not something she learned in the group—this was passive—but she felt it was the safest and easiest way to get the ball rolling. Mary didn't know why she was afraid of him. He had never hit her or scared her in any way, but she was still afraid.

After Mary told him she needed a break, she spent three days in the hospital.

When Mary, still bruised, came back to the group meeting and shared her story, Rebecca made the decision to start seeing a counselor. Her counselor was one of the women who taught the course.

What bothered Rebecca most was that Mary feared this man, but there was nothing that could be done. There was no evidence or proof that he would hurt her. He had never hurt her in the past, so she would not have been able to get a restraining order for protection. A judge wouldn't have signed it. This was a scary thought. She wondered why a person couldn't just say I'm scared and I want protection, period. If he was normal and didn't do anything, fine, but if he did try to hurt her, she would have better protection or maybe it would deter him from doing something to her in the first place.

Rebecca kept trying to deny the reasons why Roy moved in next to her. She didn't want to believe he was crazy or a borderline stalker, but she could tell he kept an eye on her. He always seemed to be in the hall when she was coming or going. He would show up in the laundry room with laundry while she was doing her laundry. Her counselor became afraid for her and told her to start documenting everything that didn't feel right. So

Rebecca bought a journal and started doing just that. She wrote in her journal every night, not only about Roy, but about what she was learning about herself. Between counseling, the women's group and journaling, she was starting to get a better understanding about the person she was and the person she wanted to be.

Her choice of men was not healthy; therefore, Rebecca was not healthy. Her job was not her dream, and she hadn't tried to do anything about it; therefore, she was discouraged. She also recognized that she had spent money foolishly while Roy was in her life. She had started shopping more and buying things she didn't need. Although she and Roy took turns paying for the dates, she usually spent more than she should have. She could no longer pay the entire balance on her credit cards at the end of the month. She was beginning to understand that her spending was directly related to being frustrated about her life and about dating Roy.

Work was also becoming more stressful. Ed was suddenly under the impression that Rebecca was a nymphomaniac, and he began making passes at her. She knew she had Roy to thank for that.

Rebecca also started having panic attacks. She didn't know if it was because she was afraid of Roy or because she was finally facing herself and all the mistakes she had made.

One night she came home from work and her panic attack was so severe that she grabbed her cordless phone and laid it on her chest and waited. She didn't know if she should call for an ambulance to come and get her. She knew it couldn't be good for her heart to pound like that for a solid hour. She turned on the TV for a distraction. Ellen was doing standup on Lifetime and Rebecca found herself laughing out loud. She wasn't sure when her heart stopped racing, but Ellen was the perfect diversion.

Rebecca continued with the group, and with her counseling, journaling and her own self-help ritual of reading self-help books from the library. After learning better communication skills from the group, Rebecca decided to confront her boss.

"I know our relationship has changed because I dated one of your best friends. I'm sorry, and I take responsibility for that mistake. But because of that, lines have been crossed and we've become more like friends than like a relationship between a boss and his assistant. I'd like to continue working with you, Ed, but I will no longer tolerate your inappropriate remarks and gestures. I'm sorry things didn't work out with your friend, but I don't want that to affect our work relationship. I'm under the impression that Roy has said things to you that makes you feel you can mistreat me. If these comments continue, I will report you to your boss. Can I continue working as your assistant and receive the respect you used to give me?"

Rebecca's boss agreed that they could continue working together and the comments would stop. And that was all that was said. Her work life improved, but her home life got worse.

One morning around three, Rebecca woke to a scraping sound coming from her kitchen. She turned on her light and the sound stopped. She knew that her kitchen wall was also Roy's kitchen wall. She turned the light off and loudly went back to her bedroom and closed the door. Rebecca stood in the hall for a minute before tiptoeing back into the kitchen. She sat on the floor and waited. After about five minutes the scraping sound started back up. She listened closely trying to figure out exactly where it was coming from.

What had led her to this point in her life, sitting on the cold linoleum floor in her kitchen wearing a t-shirt and panties, listening to see if some freaky guy was trying to come though the wall?

She quietly slid her body closer to the pantry and tried to peek under the door. She thought she could see movement. "Shit! Maybe I have a mouse," she whispered to herself. She flung open the door with every intention of looking at the floor for a mouse, but there was light coming from the wall and Rebecca made eye contact with Roy.

"I'm calling the cops!" Rebecca yelled and slammed the pantry door closed. She dialed 9-1-1.

When the police arrived, Roy was gone and there was nothing in the apartment other than a mattress on the floor. Rebecca wondered if he merely rented the place so he could spy on her. Rebecca's counselor helped her fill out the forms for a restraining order against Roy. But, the judge denied the order.

Rebecca was disappointed, but she was okay. The landlord didn't want to get involved and didn't press charges against Roy for damaging the wall, which added to her disappointment and feelings of being all alone. Rebecca felt certain that she would never see Roy again, which helped her move on with her life.

Several weeks passed, and Ed continued to treat Rebecca with respect. She wondered if her assertiveness had changed him, if Ed and Roy had had a falling out or if they had conspired to keep Rebecca working there so Ed could keep Roy informed about her. Rebecca wanted to keep her job because she wanted to deal with her other issues first. Later she would decide what to do about her career.

***

Rebecca stood up and headed to her office. When she found the card, she looked at the 'R' on the front of the little envelope again. She tore the card in half and then in fourths and tossed it into her wastebasket.

She went back into the living room and continued going through Angie's work. Rebecca learned about how slick the pimps and traffickers were when targeting girls and young women. They were going into neighborhoods and malls in the Midwest and Every Town, USA, to groom girls and young women unknowingly into prostitution.

Rebecca was thankful that she was young in a different time. Although during her high school years, she remembered being approached by a creepy man at the mall. "Could you try this shirt on for me? You are my wife's size and I'd like to see how it looks." One of the women who worked in the store overheard him and called the police. Rebecca was naive and didn't know what was going on until her sister explained it to her. She also remembered a friend being offered fifty dollars for a blowjob outside of a restaurant. She wondered how everything got so out of control.

Rebecca read about the rapes, addictions, suicides and murders of prostitutes. She learned about the devastating emotional damage and the degradation the women felt. She read about the education levels of men who use prostitutes, their marital status and the types of prostitution they use.

She also learned that most men knew it was wrong to be with a prostitute, wouldn't marry a prostitute, knew prostitutes were victims and knew prostitutes didn't make a lot of money. And most men said it wasn't okay for their daughters to be prostitutes or for their sons to use prostitutes. Most men knew that it wasn't the prostitute's choice to be a prostitute, but … most men wanted prostitution decriminalized.

Rebecca wrote, "There is a definite disconnection in society about prostitution. Should men be convicted of violence against women, and women be given mandatory help? Clearly, these women are hurting and need help. Better education? Separate education for boys and girls about these issues? Whose fault is it when we are bombarded with sex every day? We have allowed the sex industry and violence against women to become acceptable, mainstream."

Rebecca tried to imagine herself using a male escort for sex. She pictured herself picking up the phone and ordering in a man to have sex with no strings attached. She fantasized there wouldn't be strings attached, knowing there were always strings attached when it came to sex—justifying the morality of your own behavior, contracting a disease, breaking the law, hurting people, possibly being abused. Even if it were possible to have that type of exchange, Rebecca knew it was something she would never do. She would not feel good to use somebody that way, and she felt something was wrong with people who did whatever they wanted, just because they could. She felt it showed a lack of character.

The wind continued to pummel the house, causing Lily to bark, so Rebecca decided it was a good time to pop in a DVD she found in Angie's packet, *Prostitution: Beyond the Myths*. Rebecca had heard about Bill Nelson, the director of this documentary, but she didn't realize that he was Angie's friend. He was from the Minneapolis area, and he worked to help women get out of prostitution. He always said that prostitution was not the oldest profession, but the oldest way to degrade and abuse women. He demonstrated that perfectly in his documentary.

After watching the DVD, Rebecca stood up, stretched and headed to the laundry room to deal with the load of wash. She shoved the towels into the dryer and closed the laundry room door. She walked into the kitchen nook and looked out the large windows. It was dark outside and she couldn't see anything, not the moon or a single star. She hoped it wouldn't rain anymore, but she especially didn't want a thunderstorm. It seemed every time it stormed, they lost power in the house. Jack had been on a mission to get a generator, but they didn't have one yet.

Rebecca was glad Jack was out of town because sometimes her work made her angry about how some men treated women, and she didn't want to take it out on him. As she stood staring out the window, she remembered the time when she had been doing PR for a former high-priced prostitute.

*****

Holly had been saving money to better her life and get out of the business with enough money to follow her dreams of becoming a fulltime artist. While making the transition to get out, she became sick and learned that she had contracted HIV and that it had rapidly turned into AIDS.

Holly wanted to share her story and help other young women avoid her mistakes. Rebecca worked with her for a few months, helping her with her press release and coaching her on her interviewing skills. Rebecca learned a lot about the sex industry and she learned a lot about the sadness that came with it. Holly was hard and had an enormous hatred for men. But her behavior contradicted that every time she was around a man or was being interviewed by a man; the loathing was camouflaged with flirty, sexual sweetness.

Holly had been raped at a young age, so she thought that she could turn her sex into power. She convinced herself that if men were going to take it from her, she might as well sell it. She admitted that she wasted her life, wasted her brain and wasted her body, all because she didn't like herself, didn't believe she was worth more and didn't trust anyone. She said in the back of her mind she always knew that she would die of AIDS if she continued, but she couldn't stop. She didn't know how to stop.

Hatred for men had briefly colored Rebecca's life while she and Holly worked together. One evening Jack and Rebecca were lying on the couch together watching a movie. There was a scene where a man staying in a hotel called for an escort. When he was called to let him know that she had arrived, he said, "Send the bitch up," and a woman went up to his room.

Rebecca was so angry that she got up and stormed out of the room. When Jack came after her, he tried to convince her that it was only a movie. But it wasn't only a movie. That was real for so many women. And why would a woman play a role where she was a prostitute and being called a bitch?

Rebecca remembered later watching a documentary that made her understand a little better about why a woman would play a demeaning role in a movie. The documentary was about a black woman who played a maid for a white family in a television series. Many people criticized her for playing that role, and felt she was a sellout. Rebecca will never forget her reply: She said she would rather play a maid on TV than be a maid in real life.

Rebecca hoped there would be more strong female roles and better role models for women in the future—leaders and champions, not porn stars, prostitutes and victims.

9:28 PM

REBECCA JUMPED WHEN the phone rang. She checked the time. It was almost nine-thirty. Jack always called to let her know that he made it okay and to say good night.

Rebecca didn't like to fly, and she was a little nervous when Jack flew off for business. She used to make him call her as soon as he landed to let her know he made it without a plane crash, but Jack didn't like the pressure. He wanted to stay focused on work and his goals for the trip. So he said he would rather call her once he was settled in his room, relaxed and prepared for the next morning.

Rebecca didn't understand until she started traveling for business herself. She had to get her luggage, catch a cab, get to her hotel and check in, all the while mentally preparing and going over the agenda for the following day. She always forgot to call Jack as soon as she landed. His point was well taken.

"Hi, honey, I made it. I'm checked in and already in my pajamas."

"That sounds good. Oh, honey, you gave me quite a jolt this evening. You left the music on full blast again."

"Oh, Reb, I'm sorry."

"That's okay. It wouldn't have been that bad except it was rock and roll."

"Very funny. How was your day?"

"Great. How's Vancouver?

"It's rainy and gray."

"Here, too. I hope we don't get a storm."

"Oh, I have to get that generator." He sounded disappointed in himself. "Do you want me to call somebody to get a generator out there?"

"No, it's okay. It can wait. You'll be back in a couple days, and we'll do it then."

"Okay." He exhaled. "Well, honey, are you headed to bed, or are you still working?"

"I'm still working, but I'm getting tired."

"Don't stay up too late. I'll let you get back to work. I have my football game on, so I'm going to order room service and enjoy the game."

"Do they have something good or will it be your usual?"

"Funny you should ask. I was just looking at the menu and it looks like I'll be having my usual. Can't go wrong with grilled cheese."

Rebecca smiled. She knew him too well.

"But, I'm a little chilled, so I'm also going to order some soup. Bet you didn't expect that."

"Honey, you are full of surprises."

Jack laughed. "Oh, I'm in room ten-thirty-two. You have the hotel phone number, right?"

"Yes, I have it."

"Okay. Well, I'm going to say good night now so I can place my order. You know me, I'll probably fall asleep during the game. Call me if you need me, or I'll call you in the morning."

"Okay, good night."

"Good night, honey. I love you."

"I love you, too. Sleep well."

Rebecca hung up the phone and started wondering about Jack. What if he was heading to a strip bar or calling a prostitute or wanting to masturbate to pornography? Does he go to strip clubs with people from work? Does he do anything that would jeopardize their relationship? What if her husband was one of those men who takes his penis out and rubs it on women? What if she was living in denial and her husband was living a secret double life?

What if this wonderful marriage she had was a fake? What if she woke up one day with a strange, sexually transmitted disease?

Every woman must think, not my man; he wouldn't do that. Not my son. Not my dad. Not my brother. But somebody was doing it. If there was no demand, there wouldn't be so many strip clubs and prostitutes. Or was it that because there were so many women willing to demean themselves through all types of prostitution, that men effortlessly justify using and abusing women because these women are so easily accessible?

After being immersed in Angie's information, she didn't know if she should feel lucky to have such a great man or if she should be afraid and untrusting. Rebecca had always felt that trusting somebody was a wonderful quality, but she started to wonder if trust had become the same as naivety.

She started to cry. She hated doubting Jack. He had never given her a reason to doubt him, and he seemed to trust her. She could just as easily have a boyfriend come over every time he went out of town.

But doubts nibbled at her, so she decided to try to catch him doing something wrong. She would go through his office for evidence, then in forty-five minutes she would call his room. She would be able to tell if he had somebody there with him. If he wasn't in his room, then it was possible that he went to a strip club with some of the guys he worked with. That was what she would do. She wanted to be reassured that Jack was all she thought he was.

Rebecca's neck felt stiff, so she decided to do some stretches and yoga on the floor before going through his office. She took deep breaths and exhaled, releasing tension in her neck, shoulders and back. With each deep breath, she felt herself become more centered and calm. First, she smiled, then she started to laugh at her behavior and crazy thoughts. She knew that if she wanted to be suspicious, she could drive herself mad. Jack wasn't doing anything that would hurt her heart, and she wasn't going to do anything that would hurt his.

Rebecca finished her stretches, then returned once more to Angie's material. She plopped back down on the couch and began to read. She loved her career even though the world it exposed could be horrifying. Rebecca took a deep breath and hoped her next client would be a comedian.

11:20 PM

AFTER READING MORE of Angie's relentless revelations about abused women and children, Rebecca was frustrated and angry. She felt like going downstairs and lifting weights or running on the treadmill to relieve some of her anxiety. But she knew she was tired and she had been drinking, so she decided to get some fresh air and take Lily out again.

Rebecca jogged to disarm the alarm while throwing air punches. She unlocked the door, and she and Lily went outside. Rebecca stood there waiting for Lily to go while repeating, "I pity the fool who messes with me!" and "I pity the fool who messes with women!" She hadn't thought about Mr. T for a long time.

The wind had died down and the night was still and beautiful. But Rebecca's mind was racing. She had so many great ideas for Angie and how to help her. Rebecca was impressed with Angie's persistence, and she was thankful for people like Angie who had the heart and ability to make a difference. Angie was not a victim—she was a strong woman. All women have a story and all women could relate to Angie.

Lily finished and attempted to bury her potty, digging in every direction, turning and dancing around.

Rebecca laughed. "You must feel so much better, you little stinker. You are the cutest little pug in the world! Come on, let's go in where it's warm." Lily took off running for the door. Rebecca had to run to catch up so Lily wouldn't pull on the leash and choke herself. They ran inside.

Lily walked to the first step to go upstairs to bed. "You want to go to bed? Oh, okay. Let me turn off the lights and set the alarm." Rebecca went to the kitchen and set the alarm. She picked up a few more things to read, then turned off all the lights except the upstairs light. She glanced at the front door as she started up the stairs. The lock was in the vertical position—it wasn't locked. "Oh, my God!" She rushed back down and locked it.

Rebecca and Lily headed upstairs to bed. Cringing at her uneasiness, Rebecca pulled on her pajamas. Her strength and confidence had been profoundly shaken after Roy's release from prison, especially now that Jack was out of town. For the last couple of weeks Rebecca had become more sensitive to the continuous stories of rape, abduction, stalking and murder on the news. She tried to deny that she was afraid alone and overly concerned with door and window locks.

Rebecca thought about her old neighborhood and wondered when and how she had lost her courage. She wasn't afraid of anything when she was younger, and she was angry that Roy had the power to change her. She didn't want to live in fear. She wanted to be tough again—she wanted to be fearless.

At times throughout her life, Rebecca had harnessed that youthful toughness and learned to tap back into it. After the attack, she regained some of her strength and confidence after she replaced the lock on her door, started taking self-defense classes, joined a gym and started lifting weights, and installed a simple battery-powered alarm for the only window that could be accessed without a ladder.

Rebecca never wanted to be a victim again. She felt empowered by that conviction, and she hoped that when it came right down to it, she would be able to protect herself. It didn't matter if it were coyotes, Roy or a cheating husband, she hoped that she could handle anything. Which started her thinking about when she chased a burglar.

***

She and Jack were staying in a hotel in Rochester, Minnesota, where they went every year for their Mayo Clinic physicals. And every year they had the

same room, a poolside suite with a door going out to the pool and another
door that went out into the hall. Jack liked to sit out in the courtyard by the
pool every morning to read his paper and drink coffee.

They were both early risers, so one morning, still in their pajamas, they
decided to go for a quick walk around the hotel. Around five-thirty, when
they got back to their room, they were shocked by a man going through
their things. Jack tried to grab him by the arm, but he got away and took off
running. The defeated look on Jack's face and not knowing what the thief
had already stuffed into his backpack made Rebecca angry, so she kicked
off her flip flops and yelled, "Call the police!" as she took off after him.
Running as fast as she could, she chased him out of the pool area and into a
hallway. Then, not sure if her body wanted to go faster than her feet or vice
versa, she fell hard and jammed her shoulder. She was thankful she had
fallen on the carpet and not on the cement by the pool. She jumped up and
continued after him.

He ran into a fire escape stairwell; she was only one or two floors from
him. She heard a door close and she started trying to open all the doors as
she went down. The first floor door was the only one that opened, but she
saw nobody. She asked a few people if they had seen a guy wearing black
and carrying a red backpack running in this area. Nobody had. So she
headed back upstairs to the second floor using a different set of stairs. She
looked around and at the fire escape door, there it was, a bent hanger lying
on the floor. He had propped a door open for his escape. Pissed that she
hadn't caught him, Rebecca headed to the front desk where she saw Jack
and two police officers.

The cops treated her like she was too little, too weak or maybe just too
much of a woman, and she shouldn't have chased the guy; it made her
uncomfortable. She was just trying to protect herself, her husband and their
property. And maybe she'd take a bad guy off the streets for a while. The
only place the hotel had a camera was on the first floor, so they had video
of Rebecca, in her pajamas, running out of the fire escape but no pictures
of the crook. The police said they would continue checking the area.

The bellhop and front-desk workers at the hotel were amused. They
teased her, but not in a mean way. "What would you have done if you
caught him?"

"I would've beat the living shit out of him."

They laughed. Jack stood by, proud of his Rebecca. They asked Jack, "Why did you let her go after him."

"I can't stop her from doing anything she wants to do. I just said go get him, honey, I'll call the police."

Everybody laughed.

And it made it easier to laugh, too, because Jack told Rebecca that he didn't think the thief got anything, maybe a little cash. He asked her how much money she had had in her coin purse.

"I think thirty or forty dollars. Did he get my necklace?"

"Nope. We were lucky he got your thirty or forty bucks and that's it."

Rebecca was relieved. She had put her ten-thousand-dollar diamond solitaire necklace inside her coin purse. Her computer was right where the thief was standing, along with Jack's wallet and money clip with cash. They were thankful that they caught him when they did. If she had known that he only took a few bucks, she wasn't sure she would have gone after him, but in that moment nobody could have stopped her.

The next day Jack and Rebecca went for breakfast at the hotel cafe. Jack proudly told their server about Rebecca chasing the burglar. The server loved what Jack was telling her and she turned and beamed at Rebecca. Jack continued bragging. "We never saw the hotel security guards until pretty, feminine little Rebecca chases down the burglar! I can't imagine how they feel." He smiled at Rebecca. "Well, they're making their rounds now, aren't they?"

The server looked back to Rebecca. "If I had seen you chasing some guy down, I would have helped you! We'd have got him!"

***

Rebecca, smiling at the memory, had a brilliant idea. She grabbed her notes and wrote, "Join forces with Angie. Find other women and pitch full segments." She pictured all women coming together to join in the chase to stop all violence against women and children. Rebecca believed that women together were unstoppable and could change the world. The trick was to get all women to realize their worth, their strength and their endless possibilities when they worked together.

Monday
12:30 AM

REBECCA SAT UP and adjusted her pillows. Reaching for more of Angie's pages, she realized her neck and back were tight and stiff again. She did a few neck rolls, then she checked the time. Damn, she wished she had made an appointment with her chiropractor or massage therapist during business hours. A complete spa day was what she wanted, but that she would save as a reward for when she finished her work: a concrete PR plan for Angie.

Rebecca had an idea. While traveling, she and Jack often had massage therapists from the hotel spa come to the room to give them each a massage at the same time. Rebecca liked the deep-tissue therapeutic massage, and Jack liked the light massage so he could relax. Jack would always start snoring within the first few minutes of the massage, then later he would tell Rebecca that he tried to sleep but couldn't.

Rebecca went downstairs and looked in the city yellow pages under massage therapist, wondering if she could get somebody to come out to the house Monday or Tuesday, preferably a female. She knew she would have to pay more because she lived out of town, but it would be worth it. But did female massage therapists go out to people's homes at all, because it might be unsafe?

Rebecca hated how many massage businesses looked like a front for prostitution. Several would come out to the house, but they didn't look legitimate. They were not actually certified massage therapists, with some mentioning nationality or being discreet in their listings. Rebecca was taken aback—she had been naive and Angie was starting to open her eyes.

Losing interest in a massage, she closed the phone book, walked into the living room and lay down on the floor. She stretched, tightening and relaxing every muscle in her body. She heard Lily jump off the bed and come downstairs. Lily stepped up on Rebecca's chest and licked her face. "Lily," Rebecca giggled.

Suddenly, there was a loud thud and Lily started barking. Rebecca sat up quickly; stunned and afraid, she forced herself to get up and check it out. She grabbed the telephone and walked toward the sound. Lily followed, whining and huffing. Rebecca was glad she wasn't alone.

Rebecca cautiously walked down the hall and opened the main spare bedroom door. She turned on the light. Everything was in its place. The blinds were all open; she couldn't see outside, but she knew that if somebody was outside they could see in. Hating her exposure, she turned off the bedroom light, quickly walked over to the deck light switch and turned it on. One of the outside chairs was lying on its side. Her first reaction was to call the police, but as she stood there looking outside, she realized the wind had picked up again and strong gusts were coming from the west. Their outdoor furniture had been knocked around from the wind many times before. She took a deep breath, sighing in relief.

Rebecca was safe in her beautiful home. All the doors and windows were secure and she had an alarm system in place. She convinced herself that a strange noise didn't mean anything.

Rebecca went to the kitchen, poured another glass of wine and started thinking about Roy as she listened to the wind making the furniture dance around on the decks. Roy would have made a song out of it. He loved music, and she thought he should have been a musician, not a firefighter. And he had that certain oddness or depression about him that made him seem more like an artist.

On a couple of their dates Roy would start humming a song made up of the sounds around them. Although at times it bugged her, she knew he was talented and passionate about music. One night before they said good-bye, he started singing "Blue Eyes" by Elton John to her. She figured he sang that song to every blue-eyed girl he dated, but it was a nice gesture.

Rebecca hoped Roy was doing good things with his life, maybe working on his music or doing something good for himself to get his life back on track.

Rebecca suddenly ducked in fear. Somebody was knocking on the deck door off the kitchen nook. Lily started barking again. Rebecca ran into the living room, grabbed the phone and stayed hidden from that door. Her heart was racing. She checked the clock on the wall; it was a little after one. She sat down on the floor, hidden from all doors and windows to that deck. "Oh, my God!" she whispered. "Oh, my God!"

Lily was still aggressively barking at the deck door.

Rebecca could hear the wind gusts and the furniture jumping around. She heard the knock again, but it sounded different. It didn't sound like it was at the door, but like it was furniture knocking on the deck. Rebecca peeked around the wall and saw nobody at the door. Even Lily had settled down. She listened—and figured nobody had been at the door. It was just the wind.

Relieved, she leaned her head against the wall. She took a few deep breaths before stepping out from behind the wall to assure Lily and herself it was only the deck furniture being knocked around by the wind. They both mellowed out and headed back upstairs and back to work.

Rebecca stretched out on the bed with the lights on and blinds opened. She was in the country, not in the city, so she shouldn't be concerned about somebody watching her. But the open blinds made her nervous. She got up and closed them, and pushed a chair in front of the door. Now she felt secure.

Rebecca was tired. Her eyes were drooping and what she was reading wasn't registering. A little TV, she decided would take her mind away from everything else. She didn't want to think anymore tonight. Seinfeld was on—a show about nothing was exactly what she needed. Rebecca set the sleep-timer on the TV and drifted off to sleep with Lily snoring close by.

3:15AM

REBECCA WAS STAYING at her grandparents' house with her
mother, who was asleep in the upstairs bedroom. Rebecca was with Roy,
but not because she wanted to be. She was scared of him because she knew
he had murdered a woman and buried her on her grandparents' property.
Rebecca needed a moment alone so she could call the police. Roy went to
the bathroom and she ran to the phone in the kitchen, picked it up and
started to dial. Just then, he stepped next to her and watched the numbers
she was dialing. She knew he was going to kill her. She ran but he grabbed
her by the hair and she yelled, "Maaaaaaaa-ooooom!"

Rebecca woke up. It was Lily barking, not her yelling for her mother's
help. Still confused about where she was, she expected to be at her grandparents' house. The TV was off and it was dark. When she got her bearings,
she quieted Lily and listened for any strange noises. It was still windy and
Lily was upset because of the howling winds.

Rebecca lay in bed listening to the creaking house and blowing gusts.
She thought about her mom and her parents' divorce when she was young.
Her mother took off and her father raised her and her sister. Rebecca
always imagined that her mother left to be with some other guy, but it
wasn't until later she learned that her mother left for a career and was a successful broker in New York. Her relationship with her mother was always
kind of odd, Rebecca thought, because she never called her mom, never
even referred to her as her mother. She always called her Ruth, and didn't
know if Ruth asked her to call her by her name or if Rebecca chose to do

that. It was never talked about, and Rebecca didn't ask why. Ruth wasn't a great mother, but she had become a great friend and Rebecca loved her very much.

Rebecca didn't get to know Ruth until she was in her early twenties. Ruth left the family when Rebecca was six and there was little communication. Rebecca's father raised her and her sister alone, with child support from their mother. Ruth told Rebecca that she had felt tricked into marriage. She didn't want to be a mother or a wife. She wanted to travel and have a career. She wanted to earn money and have her own life. Ruth knew that Jim, Rebecca's dad, would be a great daddy to her kids, so she left to fulfill her dreams. She said she would have gone crazy if she had stayed in the marriage. She would have become severely depressed and maybe even have committed suicide.

For months Rebecca was very angry at her mother and felt unloved and unimportant. Later, Rebecca tried to understand her mother's truth, and she succeeded. They'd been friends ever since.

Rebecca also started loving her father more. She couldn't fathom the sacrifice and life changes he went through to keep and raise his daughters. Lisa never could forgive her mother and took that traditional route of children and husbands. Lisa was working to save her third marriage. But for Rebecca, Ruth inspired her to focus on her career, while her dad stressed the importance of family. Not wanting to be her mom nor her dad, Rebecca wanted to be something in the middle. Rebecca had never wanted children, but she had always wanted to be married, to have that special someone. She was a romantic, and with every man who came her way, she wondered if he would be the one. Unfortunately, she had been interested in anybody who was interested in her, and Roy was the one who made her realize that. Roy made her realize a lot of things about herself.

Rebecca had forgiven Roy. His problems had helped her find answers to some of her problems. His attack had made her do the work she needed to do to improve her life, motivating her to move in a different direction with her life and her career—one she might never had figured out on her own.

Rebecca turned the TV back on to drown out the wind. After checking the TV guide, she decided to check her TiVo; she chose "Ghost Hunters".

It took her back to thinking about her grandparents, the farm and all the fun she used to have horseback riding, baling hay with her grandpa and eating her grandma's home cooking. That farm was a constant in her life. It had been in her family her entire life, so when the farm was put on the market, Rebecca went back to stay for a few days to say goodbye. She wanted to feel close to her grandparents one more time.

Rebecca thought about her mom, dad and grandparents when her parents were still together. She often felt that her grandparents were her father's parents not her mother's. Her father's parents died young so Rebecca never knew them. Rebecca's mother's parents were very close to Rebecca's dad, and she was thankful. She also appreciated her mother for encouraging the close relationship between her own parents and her ex-husband and children.

***

The farmhouse had been sitting empty for about two years when Rebecca went to stay, and because of "Ghost Hunters," she secretly hoped she would feel her grandparents' presence at the farm. She talked to them.

Her grandparents didn't appear while she was at the farm, but one thing did happen that left the possibility open that there had been some communication or guidance from her grandma. One night Rebecca was cold and started looking for a blanket. She opened a drawer in the living-room credenza and was surprised to see one of her grandma's sweaters. Rebecca lifted the sweater to her face to smell it. The sweater didn't smell like her grandma. It smelled old and dusty. She checked the pockets and found a tissue in one of them. Her grandma always had a tissue in her pocket.

Before putting it back, she felt pulled to lift the drawer liner. She peeked under it and saw some money. The rumors were true: Rebecca had always heard that her grandmother hid money, and she wondered why. She only knew of women stashing money if they wanted to leave a bad relationship. She counted the thirty-five dollars and placed it on top of the credenza. She lifted the liner further to see if there was any more money hidden. Rebecca grabbed the envelope she saw and put the sweater back into the drawer. At first, she thought she shouldn't open it; it wasn't her business, but then thought that maybe her grandma was guiding her and there was a reason she found it.

The letter was from her dad's parents to her mom's parents and dated several years before Rebecca was born. Rebecca became very interested. Her eyes wide in disbelief, Rebecca read this three-page typed letter from somebody criticizing Ruth. The letter criticized her grandparents for raising such a strong-willed woman and criticized Ruth for being so stubborn. They feared the marriage wouldn't last and that their son was being pulled away from them. There was a hint of bribery or blackmail in the letter. Rebecca wondered why her grandma would keep something that was meant to hurt her and her family.

Folding the letter back up, she thought about what it meant. She wondered if the letter had missing pages or if there was another letter. Rebecca searched the rest of the main floor of the house but found nothing, no money, no letters.

Rebecca called Jack and read the letter to him to get his advice. Should she put the letter back? Should her sister know about it? Should she give it to her mother, her dad or should she burn it? After hearing the contents of the letter, Jack agreed it was hurtful and they decided that it wouldn't be good for anybody to know about it. They decided that she should dispose of the letter. After getting off the phone with Jack and rereading the letter, Rebecca spoke out loud, "I hope this is what you wanted, Grandma. Let me know if there is anything else."

The letter was true. Her dad had a great relationship with her mother's parents, and she didn't think he had a good relationship with his own. The marriage didn't last, and Ruth was strong willed. But the one thing she was pretty sure about was that her dad was happy, her mom was happy, and her grandparents were happy. Maybe it was different, but it worked for them. She felt sad for her dad's parents. She wondered what happened on that side of her family. Maybe she would ask her dad some day.

Rebecca thought about her own family drama. Rebecca's sister Lisa seemed to be drinking more and Rebecca was afraid she was an alcoholic. Rebecca wanted to blame Lisa's latest husband. He drank a lot and encouraged Lisa to drink with him. Rebecca didn't know how to deal with Lisa and her two teenage kids who were becoming more troubled as well. She wanted to make them realize how amazing, strong and wonderful they were, but she knew they would have to find their own way just as she had to find hers. They were growing apart and Rebecca felt bad about it. She wanted to be in their lives, but she couldn't take the drama, so she stayed away.

Rebecca had spent her share of time with people consumed with how bad their lives were and what they needed from her. She found it refreshing to talk to her mom, dad, relatives and friends who didn't live in chaos.

While watching her TiVo'd "Ghost Hunters", Rebecca cuddled Lily and drifted back to sleep and the dream about Roy continued on.

She was outside at her grandparents' house walking around the farm. Roy wanted to show Rebecca her fate. He led her to where a woman he killed had been buried by the barn. The dirt seemed fresh and one of the dead woman's high-heeled shoes was left behind in the shallow, empty grave. Somebody had moved her, but Rebecca saw exactly where the woman had been lying, her form outlined in the dirt. Roy shoved Rebecca into the empty grave and started laughing evilly.

Rebecca jerked awake. Again Lily was frantically barking, huffing and puffing and running from window to window in the bedroom and bathroom. She jumped up on the chair that was in front of the bedroom door and started growling.

"Lily, come here."

Rebecca could see light coming from outside. She hadn't closed the blinds of the windows surrounding their large jetted tub. She knew it had to be from the moon lighting the sky, but it had been cloudy and gray all day. Lily continued growling softly. Suddenly, Rebecca saw something block the light from the windows by the tub. Somebody was in her bedroom. Heat, then icy-cold shot through her body. Her throat felt full and breathing was difficult. It looked like a dark figure or a shadow walked in front of the windows. She quickly sat up, turned on the light and got out of bed.

"Hello. Is somebody there?"

Rebecca walked into the master bathroom to see if somebody was around the corner by the double sinks. Then she walked into their closet and moved the hanging clothes to see if somebody was hiding behind them. Nobody was there. She walked back by the tub and looked out the windows. The wind was blowing again and she realized that a large tree just outside the bathroom had probably caused the shadow.

She took a deep breath and exhaled. "I've watched way too many episodes of those ghost hunting shows," she said as she walked back into the bedroom. Lily was still sitting on the chair in front of the door, but instead of growling, she was wagging her tail, causing her entire body to wiggle.

"What's the problem, little stinker?"

The closer Rebecca got to Lily, the more her tail wagged. Rebecca glanced at the clock and saw it was only four-thirty. "Oh, honey, it's too early to get up now; let's try to go back to sleep."

She lifted Lily, turned off the light and got back into bed. If she didn't fall asleep within fifteen minutes, she would get up. This time she left the TV off and was sleeping soundly within minutes.

7:00 AM

THE PHONE RANG, and it was Jack calling to say good morning.

"I'm so glad you woke me," Rebecca said to Jack. "I have so much to do today and I didn't want to sleep this late."

"Glad I could help. How'd you sleep?"

"Horrible. It was really windy, lots of strange noises. I couldn't stop thinking about my grandparents, Lisa … Lily barked a lot. And when I was sleeping, I was having bizarre dreams."

"That's awful. You may need a nap today. How's the baby?"

"She's great, snuggling with me right now."

"Lucky dog."

Rebecca smiled. "How did you sleep?"

"Pretty good, the room was freezing. I couldn't get the heat to turn on. Luckily, I found an extra blanket to cover up with."

"Lucky blanket."

"I miss you."

"I miss you, too. Do you have a busy day today?"

"Meetings all day."

"Well, call me if you need a break. I'll be home."

"Not so fast. I've been thinking … I know you are very busy right now with work. We both are. So, I'd like to make an appointment with you."

"An appointment for what?"

"To make love."

Rebecca smiled. "Sounds nice."

"It's been almost two weeks. So, check your calendar and pencil me in."

"Okay, I will."

"Okay. Well, I better get going. My first meeting's in an hour. I love you."

"I love you, too. Have a good day. Bye."

Rebecca hung up the phone and went downstairs to make coffee. She took Lily outside, then fed her. Rebecca cleaned up last night's wine glass and bottle that had only a little wine left in it, and she poured a cup of coffee. All the while, she kept thinking about her dreams, wondering what they meant.

Before getting comfortable on the chaise, she reached for the remote and opened all the blinds in the living room. Then she picked up Angie's pages on addiction.

Rebecca had spent last night drinking alone, and she believed she was celebrating a few days to herself. She usually did drink the first night of Jack's business trips. But after reading Angie's information on addictions, she started questioning her own motives for having a few glasses of wine. Was she trying to numb feelings that bothered her? She read that drinking and other addictions were often used to medicate or distract oneself so one didn't have to deal with pain or feelings. She thought about her sister and wondered if she were in pain.

In her early twenties, Rebecca drank every weekend. She loved it and always had fun with her friends. In her late twenties, she began to tire of it—the same people, same bars, same stories, same hangovers. She wanted more out of life than partying. Rebecca started to enjoy work more and looked forward to maybe finding someone special to settle down with.

Rebecca was intrigued by the statistics about drinking and addictions and how it was possible to inherit those traits from parents. She hadn't realized the extent to which those behaviors could be passed down to children. Her father didn't drink at all, but her mother did and so did Jack's parents. Rebecca never thought of her mother or her in-laws as having a problem with drinking. They enjoyed a glass of wine with dinner and an occasional nightcap. Rebecca didn't remember ever seeing her mother or Jack's parents drunk.

When Rebecca walked into the kitchen for another cup of coffee, she saw a black SUV coming up the driveway. She thought about pretending she wasn't home. A few minutes later when the doorbell rang, she shut off the alarm, grabbed the telephone and hollered, "I'll get it, Jack." She dialed 9-1-1 but didn't press talk so it wouldn't connect. She answered the door and saw a neighbor who lived down the road.

"I heard somebody broke into your place," he said.

"What? No not here!"

"Oh, it must be our neighbor up on the hill."

"Somebody's place got broken into?"

"Yes, that's what my daughter said. She must have been confused about which neighbor. Or I didn't hear her right. Sorry to bother you, but I was concerned and wanted to get more information."

"How much do you know?"

"I only know that their house was burglarized and the crooks cut down one of their trees. When I get more details, I'll give you a call."

"Cut down one of their trees?"

"Yes, that's what I heard. Like I said, I'll get more information and pass it along." He walked back to his car, then turned back to Rebecca. "You know, I always hoped it would be safer out here in the country."

"Yes, I know what you mean." Rebecca noticed his wife was sitting in the car. They waved to each other.

"I guess we have these big houses … in the country … Cops can't get to us very fast. Maybe we're easy targets?"

"I guess. Do you know if it happened at night or during the day?"

"No, I'm not sure." He turned again. "I'll see what I can find out and let you know. We're going to make sure we keep our security system on; maybe you should do the same."

"Okay, thanks. We will."

"I know we live a distance apart, but we should keep our eyes open."

"I agree. I plan to. Thanks again for stopping by." Rebecca watched them pull away and went straight to the alarm system to reset it.

With her cup of coffee, Rebecca headed to her office. She went to work to meet her goal of going paperless. She used to fantasize about taking a big black garbage bag and throwing away everything in her office except her computer; she couldn't bring herself to do it. But it was a sign that she needed to clean out her files and in doing so, she found she needed only about twenty percent of the paper files she had.

While Rebecca cleaned, scanned and threw away her papers, she thought about her last trip with Jack and how it tied in with what she was learning about Angie. She had her photos on her computer and was tempted to go through them. She had over a thousand pictures and didn't want to start looking because she knew if she started she wouldn't be able to stop.

Their month-long vacation consisted of a few days in London, Istanbul and Dubai before going to Kenya and Tanzania for a twelve-day safari. After their safari, they went to Cairo for a couple days to see the Pyramids, then back to London for two nights before flying home.

Rebecca thought about the prostitute's business cards she saw in various places throughout London—a simple postcard with a naked woman in a seductive or even raunchy pose. She thought about Istanbul where she saw millions of people clogging the streets, but not one woman driving a car or out by herself walking around downtown.

In Dubai, Rebecca saw the pendulum swing too far in the opposite direction of the U.S. and she didn't know which was better—women completely covered in black and nobody allowed to take pictures of them without their permission, or men continually photographing, exploiting and making money off of young women's bodies. A relaxing day at the beach in the U.S. could land a woman on the Internet without her knowledge.

In Africa, Rebecca learned about girls' circumcision, removal of the clitoris, and how it used to be performed at age seventeen but now it was age eight. International organizations were trying to teach the tribes to stop circumcising girls altogether.

In Egypt, Rebecca was relieved that they had a female guide. The energy was different; it was good. Rebecca had always been aware of energy shifts when she was around testosterone versus estrogen. She usually preferred the estrogen unless she was with Jack or her dad.

On the trip, Rebecca learned a little about other cultures and a lot about herself. She knew how lucky she was to have been born free and raised in the United States.

2:00 PM

AS REBECCA STEPPED outside with Lily, she didn't see any coyotes or anything out of the ordinary, so they took off on their walk down the driveway. Thinking about that month long vacation, Rebecca was amazed at how well she and Jack got along during the trip. They had never been together so much without the distraction of television and friends. It was clear that they depended on each other and enjoyed each other's company—they were a good match. She missed him.

She followed the driveway along the hilly wooded area. On the other side of the house was a flat field full of tall grass and weeds. Rebecca wanted to plant lavender throughout the field to see if it would grow. She loved the color purple and adored the smell of lavender, not to mention its soothing, relaxing effect of relieving stress.

A jackrabbit jumped out from behind a tree, surprising both Rebecca and Lily. Lily started barking and wanted to chase it. Rebecca squatted down and held onto Lily as they watched the rabbit hopping around in no hurry. It was Fred, the jackrabbit that lived by them. She and Jack loved him so much they named him and started thinking of Fred as their own pet jackrabbit. They saw him often, big and beautiful and fun to watch. Fred hopped out of sight, and Rebecca and Lily continued on their walk.

Lily did her business and Rebecca picked it up with a plastic bag. She and Jack liked walking around the property holding hands and didn't want to have to worry about stepping in Lily's poop.

At the edge of the trees, Rebecca noticed a beer can lying on the ground. She stepped closer and saw a cigarette butt beside it. "That's strange." It almost appeared that somebody had been sitting there, drinking and smoking, but it was only one cigarette and one can of beer. So whoever it was wasn't there long.

Lily peed so Rebecca decided to head back toward the house and get back to work. Rebecca knew that Angie's work was making her mind race, worrying too much, thinking too much. And deep down, she didn't want to admit it to herself, but she was frightened that Roy might try to find her. When her mind was in overdrive, Rebecca knew one of the best things to do was go downstairs to the gym and work out.

Back inside, the message light was blinking on the phone. She hit play.

"Oh, hi, Rebecca. This is Harland, your neighbor. It seems the break-in might have had something to do with their kids. Seems one of them is a little troubled and has some friends who are mixed up in drugs. And they didn't have their alarm on. The sheriff thinks it's nothing to worry about, but I'm going to keep my alarm on just in case. I hope they get to the bottom of it. If I find out more, I'll let you know."

Rebecca was relieved. That was one less thing to worry about. She changed her clothes, slipped into her running shoes and went downstairs with her iPod. She set her iPod in the dock, turned up the hip-hop music, and started to work out. First things first, she thought as she started the treadmill, ready to sort through her worries so she could focus on her work and office cleanup. She took a few deep breaths and recognized that, yes, there was something wrong—her emotions were in turmoil.

Rebecca had learned a trick several years ago, and it had helped her create the life that she had and loved. Whenever something didn't feel right, she had to find its cause. Once she figured out what was bothering her, she would confront the issue or the person as quickly as possible so the problem wouldn't linger and distract her from living her life to the fullest. If the concern was out of her control or hadn't happened yet, Rebecca either let it go or made plans so she was ready for anything.

While walking on the treadmill, she started to check in with herself, probing to get to the real issue. "Am I upset that Jack is out of town?" she asked herself. "No, I'm not." Next she asked herself, "Am I hungry or tired?" and answered, "No, I don't think so." Rebecca increased the incline on the treadmill. "Okay. Am I feeling overwhelmed by Angie's work?" She didn't hesitate. "Yes, but that's my job." She thought about what she needed to do to feel better about her work. "Number one, I need to become more detached, not take things personally. Second, I need to get through her information so I can get to the fun part, the three Ps: point, purpose and pitch." Rebecca smiled thinking about the Ps. It was her favorite part of every new client. "Okay, done."

Next, she went onto Roy. "How do I feel about Roy?" Rebecca lowered the incline and slightly increased the speed. "I don't like to acknowledge my true feelings and nervousness about the possibility of Roy finding me, and wanting to hurt me. I especially hate the feeling of not knowing." Rebecca increased the speed and started a slow jog. She thought about how she could get more information about Roy. She could find out who his parole officer was and give him a call. She could call Victim Services to find out what they knew. She didn't want to make a big deal out of it, but she would rather be safe than sorry. She would rather ask the questions now than wish she had asked later. "Okay, I got it."

Rebecca made plans for what she couldn't control: burglar, coyotes and the weather. She increased the speed again and thought to herself. I'll take Lily out more frequently during the day when I can see what is going on around me. We will stay close to the house at night. If a coyote does come toward us, I'll pick up Lily and I will scream and flap my other arm like a crazy person. I will not turn my back on the coyote. I will make myself look bigger so the coyote will be more afraid of me. "Okay, done. I refuse to be afraid on my own property."

"What's next?" Rebecca said out loud. She decided that the storm moving in was related to her other fears, especially if the house lost power. She wondered if the alarm system would still work. She would call and find out when she finished working out. Rebecca knew that during almost every storm they lost power, but she didn't remember ever having the system set during those outages. Rebecca knew where the flashlights and extra batteries were. Her computer would run for a few hours so she could keep working. Also, her office phone was corded and didn't need power like most of their other phones, so her office would be a safe place to be if the power went out. She could make it fun and work by flashlight and candles. And the power wouldn't be out for long, a few hours max.

The burglar was no longer a big issue. She and Jack didn't have troubled kids, and they had an alarm system with stickers saying so in all the windows. She would arm the system at all times, especially while Jack was out of town, and she would keep all the windows and doors locked. Rebecca would stay alert. If for some reason the alarm would go off and Rebecca needed to act, she needed a plan. She decided to have a safe room, so if anything happened, she would know what to do and where to go. After much thought, she decided that her safe room would be the master bedroom. It beat out hiding in her office or trying to escape in her car because if the power went out or was cut, the garage doors wouldn't open.

She would take her cell and charger up to the bedroom in case the phone lines were tampered with. That way, she would still have a phone to call 9-1-1. If the alarm went off, she would grab Lily, head straight for their bedroom, lock the door and push the chair in front of it. "Done."

Rebecca looked around the gym for a moment and was alarmed by her own reflection. The gym had one wall of windows and three walls of mirrors. Just thinking about somebody breaking in made her nervous.

She decreased the speed on the treadmill and thought about what she should do if Roy showed up. She knew burglars would want money and valuables. But what would Roy want? Would he want to hurt her, kill her? Try to get her back? Her stomach ached. She knew he would want to hurt her. Roy had been in prison, and people say that you learn more about crime in prison than anywhere else. That thought frightened her. What if he knew how to break in or disarm the alarm without detection? Rebecca decided that wasn't possible with today's technology.

"Okay," she said and increased the speed and incline of the treadmill again. "Everything is good." She spent the next fifteen minutes at a slow jog. Her mind cleared, and she felt strong and powerful. She didn't need to be afraid.

When Rebecca started her cool down, Lily jumped on the treadmill and walked between Rebecca's legs. This was the routine they had started when Lily was a puppy. Lily was always proud walking with Rebecca. Whether they were outside or on the treadmill, she held her head high while her little ears bounced. Lily could always make Rebecca giggle.

Finished with her cardio cool down, she hit the switch for the steam room and glanced inside to make sure it was working. The steam room hadn't been used for a while. She went back to the bench to do a few sets of abs: crunches and leg lifts.

Rebecca was feeling good. She danced around to her music while she lifted weights. She did a few dumbbell curls and started thinking about Roy and the part he had played in her life. It was he who made her fix her life. Roy was the worst in the mix of her failed relationships, but he forced her to face the fact that she had been the common denominator in the lives of the men she dated. She couldn't keep blaming the guys. She had to take a look at herself and her choices in men. She wondered if Roy had helped her more or hurt her more. As much as it sucked to be afraid, she knew every-thing happened for a reason. Maybe Roy was a lesson she needed to learn. She never would have found love like she had with Jack if Roy hadn't come along.

She finished working her back, biceps and abs, before heading to the steam room. She took off her clothing, stepped inside and closed the door behind her. The moist heat felt amazing and she smiled as the thick steam enveloped her. She thought about the weekend she met Jack.

***

She had taken Friday and Monday off work, personal days, and headed to Denver for a getaway, Thursday through Sunday night. Her long weekend of shopping, nice restaurants and spa treatments filled Rebecca with excitement, and she knew the change of scenery would be good for her. She had never done anything so spectacular for herself before, but one of the books she was reading encouraged her to love and treat herself like she was important. This trip was also a reward for getting back on track with her finances; over the last few weeks, Rebecca had been working overtime to get out of debt.

From the women's group, counseling and reading self-help books, Rebecca decided that she wanted to celebrate her freedom from men for a year. She knew that by freeing up her time, she could spend more time with family and friends, find her dream career, and learn more about herself and why she settled for unhealthy men. When she was ready to start dating again, *she* would do the picking and he would have to be perfect for her.

Getting to the hotel later than anticipated, Rebecca ordered room service. After she ate, she hung her morning breakfast order on her door, and snuggled into bed to watch TV. She was excited about the next morning's spa experience. She woke to her morning order being delivered, fruit, yogurt and a crescent roll. She felt like she was being served breakfast in bed.

At seven, she jumped in the shower to get ready for a little shopping before her spa appointment. The water pressure was awesome and she didn't want to get out from under the hot water. She dried off and lay back down on the bed, the white sheets feeling so fresh and new. She could smell her perfume from the night before and hugged a pillow to her body. Rebecca was happy. She was alone and happy.

After successfully shopping at one of the hotel boutiques, Rebecca was relaxing and getting a pedicure when a peculiarly attractive man came in. He nodded to her and sat down next to her for a pedicure. Rebecca was paging through some of her notes and ideas she had about starting her own PR firm. This, she had discovered, was her ultimate goal. She woke up that morning knowing that PR was her mission, her dream and her purpose. She also knew that she wanted to focus on women.

Rebecca chose a deep, dark red for her toenails to match her freshly painted fingernails. She figured she needed some fire and passion in her life—not with a man, but with herself and her future.

The man sitting next to her began talking loudly on his cell phone as if he wanted everybody to hear his conversation and she was sure everybody did, even the people getting massages and facials in different rooms. She thought somebody should tell him to be quiet. Wasn't this supposed to be a place to relax? Nobody wanted to hear about his latest business deals. Were cell phones even allowed in spas? She started to get the feeling that he was a regular at the spa and nobody seemed to want to tell him to keep it down. So she decided she would.

Once he was off the phone, Rebecca commented, "You're a loud talker."

The two women giving the pedicures tried to hide their shock and laughter.

He immediately started laughing and turned toward her, interested in what she had to say. "Is that right?"

She continued to focus on her work and didn't look up. "Yes."

"Have you ever known one of us loud talkers?"

"No."

"Well, then, my name is Jack." He reached out his hand to shake hers.

"Rebecca." She looked at her nails, gave them a quick blow and lightly shook his hand, showing little interest in continuing the conversation. Rebecca's pedicure was finished, and it was time for her facial. As she was helped out of the chair, she heard Jack say, "It was nice to meet you, Rebecca."

Rebecca turned and smiled back at Jack, flattered but not interested. This trip was for her and about her. A man would just get in the way.

After her day of being pampered, she showered and put on the new cashmere lounge suit she bought that morning. She wasn't sure what she would do with the rest of her evening, but she was eager to get back to her hotel room. She went to the front counter of the spa to pay for her treatments. She stood waiting while the man working the desk finished his phone call. She could tell he was getting her bill together for her, so she reached for her wallet and waited.

"Okay, we'll see you on Tuesday at eleven o'clock. Thank you," he said before hanging up the phone. "Okay. Let's see. You had a manicure, pedicure, facial and massage."

"That's right. And it was wonderful."

"Well, I'm glad you enjoyed yourself. Would you like to bill this to your room? Oh, wait a minute, it has been taken care of."

"Um, no. I ... I haven't paid yet."

"Yes, a gentleman named Jack took care of your bill."

"You're kidding me?" Rebecca was shocked. "Is he still here?"

"No, he left after his pedicure."

"Well then …" Rebecca stared at the wall fountain behind the desk. She shook her head in disbelief and started to put her wallet away. "Oh, I'd like to tip …"

He interrupted, "It's been taken care of."

Rebecca put her wallet in her bag, said thanks and went back to her hotel room. Feeling a little uneasy, she tried not to think about it, but her curiosity about this man kept growing. She didn't know anything about him, just that he was a loud talker named Jack. She wondered if he knew her last name or if he got it when he paid her bill. Would she ever see or hear from him or was it just a random act of kindness? She shook her head, hoping to clear her thoughts of him. This trip was about her alone.

4:05 PM

WHEN REBECCA GOT out of the shower, she wanted to wear the same cashmere outfit she bought the weekend she met Jack. It wasn't in the changing room so she threw her towel in the dirty clothes basket and started up the stairs naked. As she walked quickly up the stairs, she became acutely conscious of her nakedness. She felt powerless and like she was being watched. But she always felt more vulnerable when she was naked. She wondered what it felt like for strippers and women in pornography.

About halfway up the stairs, she heard a loud crack and bang. She stood still. Lily started barking. The thunder rumbled loudly outside. She looked up the stairs, then continued walking. She glanced toward the windows and saw the sky changing. Dark clouds surrounded the house. "Oh, God, please don't let the power go out." Just as she said that, there was another loud crack and Lily barked again. The lights flickered.

"Honey, it's okay. It's just thunder."

Rebecca rushed up the next set of stairs to the third floor and into the master bedroom closet. She pulled out the camel-colored cashmere lounge suit, held it up to her face and smelled it. She smiled and quickly got into it. It seemed a little tighter than it used to. "Oh, well." She hugged herself as she headed back downstairs. She glanced at the clock. It was just after four in the afternoon but almost dark outside because of the heavy clouds.

Rebecca went straight to the kitchen and picked up the phone. She dialed the home security's number, and asked, "If the power goes out while the alarm system is armed, what will happen?" Rebecca was assured a backup system was in place. She would hear a solid tone until the system was restored and rearmed, which usually took less than thirty seconds. Rebecca felt much more secure.

She sat on the deep sofa watching the rain and anticipating each rumbling of thunder. The clouds were thick and heavy. The thunder was loud, but infrequent and there wasn't much lightning. Her mind drifted back to that weekend she met Jack.

***

She had returned to work the following Tuesday, and she gave Ed a month's notice. She was nervous about quitting but knew she had to make changes in her life. She had to go for her dreams, and she needed the pressure of deadlines and timetables. Rebecca started phoning PR firms to see if they needed help in their office. She wanted to at least get her foot in the door.

After a few days, Response Public Relations, a PR firm just starting out, called back. Three women in the office needed help with answering phones, making calls, doing computer work, cleaning the office, researching clients, filing, and there was room for advancement. It was perfect. She drove to Denver for the interview and was hired on the spot. Rebecca would start by working from home until she felt she could leave her other job and move to Denver. She couldn't believe how everything was working out. Happy and excited, Rebecca called her mother in New York to tell her the great news.

That weekend, Rebecca went to Cheyenne to spend time with some friends. She had planned to stay both Friday and Saturday nights, but on Saturday night she felt an urgent need go back home. When she entered her apartment, Roy attacked her.

Rebecca was thankful to have a counselor and support in place. She had already been focusing on how to better herself and her life, so as devastating as the attack was, Rebecca was able to move on quickly. She worked with Victim Services, found answers that she needed and became her own best advocate. She was sometimes anxious about Roy, but she would not let this experience destroy her, and she was more excited than ever to move and leave her past behind.

During Rebecca's last week in Fort Collins, she said goodbye to friends from her group, her counselor and some of her old coworkers. Although Fort Collins was not far from Denver, she knew that she would be busy, and she wasn't sure she would want to return to that part of her life. Her direction was forward to her new apartment and her new career.

Two days before she moved to Denver, her phone rang. It was Jack.

"You're not easy to track down."

"Who is this?"

"Jack ... the loud talker."

"Jack! Thank you for paying for my spa day!"

"You're welcome. So you live in Fort Collins."

"Actually, I'm moving to Denver in two days, for work."

"That's wonderful. How about after you get settled, you give me a call and we'll have dinner."

"Sure that sounds nice." She pretended to write down his number and they said their good-byes. She knew she wouldn't call him. She also knew she was being passive, but she wasn't perfect. She didn't want to explain her life to this stranger, Jack. Rebecca sat in her packed-up apartment ready for change but not ready for another man.

4:35 PM

REBECCA STOOD UP from the couch and realized she was hungry. She headed into the kitchen to make her favorite meal and the only thing she knew how to make, pasta. She filled the pot with water and placed it on the burner. She stepped into the pantry for the pasta that she always had on hand. She pulled out a handful and broke it in half before setting it into the water.

Loud thunder roared through the valley and the house shook. She tensed and waited for the power to go out, but it didn't.

Rebecca grabbed a bottle of water from the refrigerator and gulped down a third of it. She knew she needed to drink more water; she would work on that. Rebecca felt invigorated and alive. She was physically and mentally stronger than she had been before her workout and self-check-in. Now she had a plan for everything.

Rebecca knew that in all probability Roy most likely wouldn't come after her and she had to stop thinking about him so much. If he skipped out on seeing his parole officer, she was certain that she would be notified. If that happened, she would allow herself to worry, and she would ask Jack to come home or she would get a bodyguard. Rebecca decided not to call Victim Services or try to contact his parole officer.

Rebecca rinsed the pasta, then added butter and parmesan cheese. Taking a fork from the drawer, she sat down in the kitchen nook. Her thoughts drifted back to Jack while she ate.

Jack had always made her feel safe in every way. But there was something she never considered about him before—he wanted everybody to be safe. Maybe that was the sign of a great man. Rebecca remembered all the little things he did for others.

Once they were in the Bahamas having breakfast, and there was a younger couple just a few tables away who seemed concerned about the bill and their lack of money. Jack told the server to put their bill on his.

Jack also took good care of his two, more serious, ex-girlfriends after they broke up. He helped pay for school for one, and helped out the other financially when she had some health issues and struggled to pay her bills. At first, it bothered Rebecca, but later she understood that was just who Jack was, and she admired him.

Then there was Melvin from just a few days ago when Jack was getting an oil change. An older man sat down and started talking to him. Melvin told Jack about his financial trouble and how he needed to drive over two thousand miles across country to get back home. The mechanic came over and told Melvin that he needed a few things done and four new tires. Jack followed the mechanic to the shop and told him that he wanted to buy the four new tires for Melvin anonymously. So he did. Later Jack noticed that the mechanic had written on his bill, "Jack bought Melvin four new tires so Melvin could make his trip home. God bless you."

Tears welled in Rebecca's eyes.

She was feeling tired, which often made her more emotional, so she decided to get back to work. She turned on the fireplace and sat down to find out more about Angie. Rebecca read two more eye-opening articles: "Why Prostitution Should Not be Legalized" and "Violence Against Women and Children: How it Affects Everybody."

Rebecca understood that it was all connected: child sexual abuse, domestic abuse, addictions, rape, strippers, prostitution, pornography, the overall lack of value placed on people. "Empowered women make healthier choices," Rebecca wrote in her notes.

Rebecca knew that when she felt strong, happy, loved and empowered, she made better choices in her life. But when she was feeling lonely, depressed, inadequate or rejected, she often made poor choices.

Returning from the kitchen with a Diet Coke, she continued reading where she left off. Lily jumped up to lie next to her, grunting several times while she got comfortable. "You grunt like an old man," Rebecca said and rubbed Lily's side.

Angie had charts and diagrams about how little girls get sucked into the cycle of abuse and how sex predators work. The charts were very interesting and easy to follow and understand. Her chart on sex crimes listed the types of crimes, the ages of the perpetrator versus the ages of the victim, and what the punishment was. Angie wanted a national law so that parents living in Wisconsin would have a better understanding of what type of crime their sex offender neighbor from Texas committed. The language, crime and punishment needed to be the same in every state across the country.

Angie included a copy of her letter to politicians and organizations that could help. The letter discussed her goal to have a consistent national database for sex offenders and to have this chart she created, or something similar, mailed to every household so every U.S. citizen would clearly know what was a crime and what wasn't. She wanted parents to talk to their kids about date rape and appropriate ages of boyfriends and girlfriends. She wanted parents to talk to their kids about their own bodies and how to protect them. She wanted to expose child sexual abuse and get help for children, even if it was the inner child of a grown woman who had been assaulted; it didn't matter how long ago it happened. Angie wanted to instill in everyone the importance of telling somebody, getting help and getting the perpetrator off the street.

Rebecca realized after going through more of Angie's things that there were national laws in place to help and protect women and children, but they were not enough. There were such laws as Amber Alert, Megan's Law, the Violence Against Women Act, and the Adam Walsh Child Protection and Safety Act. Angie's ideas were similar to the Adam Walsh Child Protection and Safety Act. Unfortunately, laws didn't mean much when there wasn't enough funding to support them.

Rebecca read Angie's letters of rejection, everybody from America's Most Wanted to Congress. Most agreed with her, but said each state had its own system of funding, laws and language. Rebecca didn't realize that. She figured when dealing with children concerning perpetrators who could drive or fly from state to state that the laws would be the same throughout. Rebecca was feeling as discouraged as Angie probably had been. She got up and headed to her office to find out more about these laws to protect women and children.

After researching national laws and looking for sex predators on the Internet, Rebecca called her sister to tell her to check her neighborhood. Rebecca found many sex offenders listed in the area her sister lived in, which also wasn't far from her dad's house and the neighborhood where she grew up. She checked her area and her mother's area; both were clear.

Rebecca knew how lucky she was to have Jack, and she knew that money had bought her security. Money seemed to buy safety, and that was a topic she kept coming back to while reading Angie's materials and thinking about the lives of other women.

Rebecca lay down on the couch to sort out her thoughts about Angie and fell asleep. She woke when Jack called her to say good night around nine-thirty. She was glad he woke her.

"So ... when is our appointment?"

Rebecca laughed nervously. "Honey, I'm sorry. When do you get in on Thursday?"

"Late. That's why I'm taking a town car."

"How late? I'll wait up for you."

"I'm scheduled to get in around ten-thirty-five. And by the time I get home it will be about twelve-thirty."

"Okay, you're penciled in. Twelve-thirty Thursday night."

"Looking forward to it."

"Me too." Rebecca started getting excited. Just the thought of having his body against her and his hands caressing her skin caused her breathing to change. Her head felt light.

After hanging up the phone, she started creating the fantasy in her mind; it would be their first time. Jack was her new boyfriend and he was coming to stay for a visit. She had desperately wanted him since they met and she knew that Thursday night would be the night they would make love for the first time.

She wondered what he would be like. Would he be good? Would he feel good inside of her? How many times and for how long would they make love?

Rebecca felt giddy and excited. Her "first time" fantasies were her favorite. She was a romantic who loved the first kiss, the first touch and the first time. And Rebecca had many first times with Jack, but he didn't know about it. She kept her fantasy to herself.

Men weren't the only ones who joked about being with the same person for the rest of their lives. Women sometimes dreaded that thought too.

Rebecca had heard too many of her friends who had been married for years talk about never having another first kiss, first date or that first time a man reaches for their hand. But especially there was that talk about never having the excitement of the first time again. The way they talked about it made her fear some of her friends were contemplating adultery.

Rebecca would always secretly have first times with Jack for the rest of her life, and she couldn't wait.

It had stormed most of the day, but the power stayed on. As she looked outside she could see that the rain had been replaced with a lightning storm. "What strange weather." She decided to take Lily out while there wasn't much rain.

"Lily, come on baby. You wanna go outside?" Lily was lying on the floor by Rebecca's feet. Rebecca gently patted Lily and lifted her up. Seeing the alarm note, she went back to the kitchen to disarm the alarm. Rebecca yawned and slipped into her shoes. She attached Lily's leash to her harness, and she opened the front door. It was pitch black. Rebecca stepped back in and turned on all the outdoor lights. "Now hurry, honey. Mama doesn't like this weather." She closed the door behind them.

The night air was chilly, but it wasn't raining. The grass was wet and slippery under Rebecca's shoes. "Hurry up, honey." Lily sniffed around, and Rebecca kept looking toward the trees going up the hill. Because she couldn't see anything in the distance, she listened intently, too.

Lily started turning in circles, her ritual before peeing. Then she quickly squatted. Just as she was finishing, Lily started barking into the darkness.

Rebecca looked in the same direction but saw nothing. "It's okay, honey." Each lightening strike terrified Rebecca. She could see everything in that instant, but then everything went black again. It was eerie, and Rebecca still felt as though she were being watched.

Lily continued looking around, then sniffing the grass. Another lightening strike and Rebecca thought she saw something in the distance, but then it was dark again. Her eyes readjusted to the darkness. The next strike came suddenly and felt so close Rebecca cried out, "Baby, let's go inside," as she ran toward the door. Rebecca didn't want to see coyotes or anything else coming out of the darkness. Once back inside, she didn't feel as afraid with the door locked and the alarm on.

Rebecca was cold and plopped down in Jack's soft leather chair in the living room. She could smell his cologne, Fahrenheit, and it took her back to how they finally ended up together.

***

Despite the lingering fear of not knowing where Roy was, her life was right on track. Rebecca was debt free, working on her career with the goal to help other women through public relations. She was picky about friends and because of that she noticed that only great people started to show up. When Jack came along the third time, she was healthy and ready for him.

Only a few months had passed, but Rebecca was settled into her new job and new apartment. She loved her life. One evening after coming home from the apartment complex gym, her security buzzer rang. It was Jack. She let him in and a couple minutes later, he was knocking at her door. She looked out her peephole and unlatched the lock. He was holding a small sterling silver candleholder shaped like a heart with a candle inside.

He handed it to her. "A late house-warming gift."

Rebecca smiled. "Thank you. Would you like to sit down?" She led him to the couch as she smelled the vanilla-scented candle, a scent she loved.

"Sure." He sat down and looked around. "Nice place."

"Thanks, I love it here."

"Have you eaten?"

"No, actually I haven't."

"Would you like to go and get something together?"

"How does Italian sound? There's a place across the street."

"That sounds great."

"I just came from the gym and I'd like to freshen up a little and change. Can I meet you there in fifteen minutes?"

Jack looked at her and raised his eyebrow. "Are you really going to meet me or are you going to leave me sitting there?"

"I'll be there in fifteen minutes."

Jack left, and Rebecca rushed into the bathroom to wash up and then into her bedroom to change. She was out the door in ten minutes and saw him standing at the bar watching a basketball game. As soon as he saw her, he walked toward her and guided her to their table. Jack was a gentleman. He had her walk in front of him, he helped her with her jacket, but he didn't overdo it by helping her with her chair. Rebecca liked him, but she was being cautious, nervous about getting involved with another unhealthy man. But Rebecca felt better prepared and didn't want to doubt every man who entered her life. She didn't want to be afraid.

"How do you like living in Denver?"

"I love it. I love the city."

"Do you mind if I ask what you do for a living?"

"Well, that's a good question … I answer phones, file, make phone calls, make coffee, go grocery shopping, oh, and I clean bathrooms."

He looked a little confused. "You don't sound happy."

"I guess I'm in between something, I'm just not sure what yet. I'm in the process of doing PR. That is what I want to do, but I'm just starting out and working at a PR firm right now, I guess you could say as the … secretary?" Rebecca's face crinkled in confusion.

Jack started laughing. "Oh, Rebecca, I've been there many times."

She liked how he said her name. He said it like they had known each other for years.

"What do you do, Jack?"

"Let's just say, it's an interesting time working in oil and gas. I recently sold my business and did … well for myself." He smiled. "Now I do some consulting on the side and I'm working on a few other projects."

"Do you live here in Denver?"

"I do, but I travel a lot, usually Texas and lately up north to Canada. I used to travel more overseas, Middle East, but I would like to settle down a little."

"That sounds exciting. I love to travel, though I haven't done much. I've traveled around the U.S. a little with family and friends but that's about it."

"Then join me on my next trip to Canada. I work most of the day, but you could do some sightseeing. Do you have your passport?"

"I do. I was actually planning a trip to Canada or Mexico. I'm ready to travel beyond the U.S., and I thought a connecting country would be my next step."

"That makes perfect sense to me."

Rebecca was surprised by Jack's invitation coming so quickly. He didn't even know her. She figured it was just something nice to say, that he couldn't be serious.

Rebecca had a wonderful dinner with Jack and hoped he did, too. On the walk back to Rebecca's apartment, Jack asked her if he could call her again. She said she would like that. He asked about her ditching him the first time around, and she just explained that the timing was off. She was in a better place now. He understood.

At the door, Jack leaned in for the kiss and Rebecca let him. His kiss was confident and passionate, his lips soft, yet strong. This loud-talking man had suddenly gone quiet and was trembling. Rebecca started to feel something she had never felt before, something in her heart. His kiss was perfect. And though her body didn't go crazy, her mind did. She really liked him. She felt something, something amazing. She wanted him to kiss her again, but he didn't.

She reached her hand out to shake his. "Thank you for a nice night."

He looked confused by her extended hand. "We just kissed good night."

"Oh." She turned to let herself into her apartment, but her door was still locked and she hit her head against the door. "Ouch." She reached up to put her hand against her forehead.

"Are you okay?"

"No ... I'm embarrassed." She took a deep breath. "I didn't expect your kiss to be so ... so perfect."

He smiled. "Okay then, Miss Rebecca. Have a good night." He reached his hand out to shake hers.

They shook hands.

"I'd like to end this on a good note. Thanks for having dinner with me."

"Thanks for asking … again."

Before they released hands Jack kissed hers. Rebecca unlocked her door and went inside.

***

Rebecca got up from Jack's chair with a huge smile on her face. She loved her life, and Jack was the greatest man she had ever known, besides her dad. Jack wasn't perfect, but he was perfect for her. He was respectful, trusting, kind and supportive of her and everything she did.

When she went to the laundry room to take out the towels, she looked out the window and saw the rain really coming down again. Only an occasional lightening flash lit the sky and the thunder had quieted to a dull grumble. Rain had been coming down off and on all day, and now it was getting cold. She wondered if it ever hailed at night. She only remembered it hailing when it was light outside.

She finished folding the towels then wiped off the kitchen counters and table. Lily would have to go outside again before bed; she still had to go number two. Rebecca wouldn't even attempt to take Lily out in the rain, because the second rain hit Lily's face, she would take off running back to the front door. Sometimes Rebecca wished she would just go in the house. Number two would be easy to pick up and flush.

Rebecca decided to make herself an espresso because she wanted to get more work done before bed. Even though she already knew everything she needed to know about Angie and her work, she was afraid she might miss something. She knew Angie had a general idea about who she was and what she was doing, but it was Rebecca's job to come up with what was saleable to the media and public, what they wanted and needed from Angie.

Making an espresso always reminded Rebecca about the cruise she and Jack took to Bermuda. Their butler kept asking them if they wanted an espresso; neither Jack nor Rebecca had tried an espresso before, so the first two days of their cruise they said no. But on the third day, feeling a little sluggish, they agreed to have an espresso—they were hooked. Jack bought an espresso machine when they returned from the trip.

As Rebecca finished making her vanilla espresso, she heard Lily scratching and barking at the front door.

"Oh, no, Lily." Rebecca looked outside then turned to talk to Lily, "Lily, honey we were just out there. Why now, when it's pouring?" She looked back out at the lightning and heavy rain coming down. Sighing, she said, "I'd only do this for you. Come on," and slipped on her jacket and shoes, then grabbed Lily's leash. "Lily, sit." Rebecca attached the leash. "Oh, wait a minute." She ran through the kitchen to the garage door with Lily jumping at her legs. She turned off the alarm and walked back to the front door. She took another glance out the window. "Are you sure you can't wait?"

Lily tilted her head to the side knowing Rebecca was talking directly to her.

"You are so cute. Let's go." She opened the front door and stepped into the rain. "Lily, you need to be quick about this. We don't want to get struck by lightning."

In the yard, Lily sniffed around for a minute but was more interested in looking up at the rain, then lifting her paws to wipe her eyes from the rain hitting them.

"Hurry up!" She gave a quick tug to the leash.

A loud thunder crashed and Lily started barking.

"Lily, hurry up!" Rebecca was starting to get scared. She decided to walk a little farther out into the yard to get Lily moving around, hoping she'd remember why they were outside.

Lightning flashed to the right of her, and in that moment she thought she saw somebody leaning up against the garage. Rebecca was in shock and couldn't move. She waited for the next lightning flash to look again. There was nobody there. Her heart settled down, and she giggled to herself just as she noticed Lily squatting. "Oh, thank God." She couldn't believe how nervous she was alone in dark, stormy weather. Lily finished her business and took off running for the door. Rebecca ran after her with her head down to avoid the rain in her face. "Good girl!" she yelled as they ran. She would pick it up in the morning.

They were soaked. Rebecca threw her wet jacket onto the bench by the door as she headed to the kitchen to reset the alarm, then both headed straight to the fireplace. Lily pulled a green ape from her toy box, and Rebecca played tug-of-war with her for a few minutes, before sipping her espresso and getting back to work.

Rebecca's thoughts returned to Bermuda again where they had leased a sailboat to take them around the island.

***

The captain was a pig. He started talking about going to the U.S. and going to "titty bars." Jack stopped him and he apologized. Later the captain told them that whenever just a single couple chartered the boat, he knew it was so the woman could sunbath topless, which he constantly let Jack and Rebecca know he was fine with. He said he always left his co-captain home so the couple would feel more comfortable.

To get away from the captain, they went to the front of the boat where there was a pad to stretch out on. They lay facing each other and Jack held Rebecca's hand. After a moment of quietly looking into each other's eyes, Jack said, "Aren't you going to take your top off?"

***

Just as she had that day on the sailboat, Rebecca burst out laughing and started thinking about Angie and her story. "Oh, the experiences we women have!" She hoped she could make the connection between Angie and other women who were making a difference or who had been victims and not only survived, but thrived in their lives.

Just such a woman was Leslie, a woman she recently helped promote. Leslie had produced and directed a documentary about her road trip across the United States. It was called *Sunset to Wonder: All Women's Journey across the United States.* Rebecca loved it. The documentary actually began in Sunset, Florida, close to Miami, and ended in Wonder, Oregon, close to the west coast. The documentary's opening shot was a homeless man standing in the middle of the road blocking a Mercedes from driving. The homeless man

was trying to get some money from the rich man. Leslie captured unbeliev-
able footage, filming all the fancy expensive cars, then two blocks later, a
homeless shelter in Miami where there wasn't enough room to house all of
the homeless. They were lying on the sidewalks and standing on the corners
with their belongings. Women were prostituting themselves, walking
around in dirty, raggedy bras and short shorts or underwear.

When Leslie started the filming, she wanted to document extreme
poverty versus great wealth in the United States. Leslie realized that there
was something deeper going on, and until women were treated better, there
would always be poverty. Leslie's filming started to document this reality.
Although poverty wasn't in your face everywhere, women being treated as
objects was in your face and it was everywhere. Leslie videographed cars,
trucks, vans and cabs with paintings, banners and advertisements for strip
clubs, Hooters, adult video and toy stores, and other businesses using
women to sell their product, everything from women's thighs, to women's
cleavage and butts. There were large billboards along the highways, both in
small towns and in large cities, advertising the same types of degradation of
women.

Leslie was brave enough to stop at some of these strip clubs, adult
stores and massage parlors along the highways to talk to women, and some
of them were brave enough to talk to her on film. Sometimes Leslie had to
pay for their time. Although these women didn't always give the answers
Leslie believed to be true, it was obvious that the women were hurting
under their tough exteriors and were possibly being controlled by traffickers, pimps and prostitution rings.

Leslie felt that some of her most dangerous filming occurred when she
filmed men walking into those places. She filmed openly, but often from
her vehicle so she could get away quickly. She said she wanted them to see
her doing it so she could get a response from them, a reaction. And she
always did. The men did not want her filming them. Some became angry
and Leslie would just remind them of the First Amendment and that they
were in a public place.

Leslie's journey consisted of truckers honking at her for no reason, the
Don Imus controversy playing out on the radio, overnight stays at hotels
that had pornography in the rooms and escort ads in the phonebooks.

During late night TV on the big network channels, she recorded some of the Girls Gone Wild ads and nine-hundred numbers being advertised by women in lingerie.

Leslie clearly showed how toll highways didn't have the billboards and ads for strip clubs, adult stores and massage parlors. Money seemed to clean up and clean out the seedy businesses and advertisements. When Leslie was on highways with the degrading messages, she said she felt angry, tense; she didn't feel proud to be a woman. But when she was driving on toll roads, she felt safe, happy and good about herself.

During her documentary Leslie made a plea to women in the sex industry. "I know you are hurting. And I know this isn't always your choice, but there is help out there. Please talk to somebody. I know you want and need money, but this kind of money doesn't buy security; it buys danger. Making this choice so you can have money is like deciding to walk into fire so you can avoid getting burned. Please trust you are worth more. I know you are worth so much more."

Imagining Angie and Leslie working together, Rebecca took a few notes.

After Leslie's road trip, she started working on another documentary to help women. One episode was about an eye-opening experience on a plane from Miami to Boston. Leslie was sitting in first class, and the plane was preparing to land. A little girl a few seats back in coach started to cry. Leslie knew that her ears were probably bothering her, and she wasn't old enough to understand why. The mother was doing all she could to quiet her baby. Leslie heard a man, sitting directly behind her, getting very upset. He kept mouthing off about the "crying brat." He was loud and obnoxious, and she hoped the mother couldn't hear him. Then he said, "Why can't she shut the little bitch up!"

Leslie was furious when she heard that comment from a grown man. She knew if she didn't say something to him, she would regret it for the rest of her life. So when the plane landed and everybody was reaching for their luggage in the overhead compartment, Leslie looked at him and said, "That is really inappropriate to call a three-year-old a bitch."

He said, "I call 'em like I see 'em."

"I think *you* should take a look in the mirror." Leslie said, and that was the end of it. She had had the last word.

Not long after that incident, Leslie started a Stop the B-Word Campaign. She used the acronym BWORD: Being Women Of Respect and Dignity and Because We're Optimistic in Reversing the Damage. She started the campaign to encourage women to be mindful of the B-Word and the impact it makes on all of us. Her website stated:

We have high hopes that we can change the frequency by discouraging the use of this degrading word against women. We are offering a sign-up sheet for anyone willing to do one or all five from this list:

- *Personally make the decision to stop using the B-Word.*
- *Invite your daughter to stop using the B-Word and to sign the sheet. (This could be a great mother–daughter bonding and communication tool, teaching the importance of being a young woman of dignity and respect.)*
- *Make your home a B-Word-free environment.*
- *Tell the men in your life (husband, sons, father, friends) to stop using the B-Word around you.*
- *Encourage your friends to stop using the B-Word and to sign up for our campaign.*

Give yourself a hug if you have already eliminated the B-Word from your life, but please sign up to help support the rest of us. By signing, you will be kept updated on how we are doing with signatures and how many brave men have joined us.

It's said that if women lead, men will follow … Let's see what we can do together.

And Leslie was proud to relay the message to women that, "For anyone who has lost faith in men, I just want you to know that we have just as many men signing up for our Stop the B-Word campaign as we do women."

Leslie learned as much as she could about the injustices toward women like how women drive much more than men, but airbags in cars were designed to save the average-sized man, not the average-sized woman. She uncovered more about women's heart disease, the symptoms and other issues regarding women's health. She learned how eighty-seven percent of cosmetic surgery is performed on women and how women who have breast implants are three times more likely to commit suicide.

She pointed out how the photos in newspapers were about seventy-nine percent men and twenty-one percent women though women make up fifty-one percent of the population. She wondered what messages were being sent: that women are only twenty-one percent important? She also noted that the majority of the photos of women were women as victims or women in the background: the passenger in the car, not the driver; the nurse, not the doctor; the wife of the president, not the president.

Leslie talked about the roles of women on TV and in movies, commercials and cartoons. She had seen too many coaches call men a bunch of girls or women as an insult. Is it an insult to be female? She was tired of romantic movies being called chick flicks or women's literature being called chick lit. Would it ever be okay to call men's literature dude lit? These messages demean and degrade women.

Leslie documented herself making phone calls and writing letters to the media, advertisers and organizations, sometimes boycotting their event or product, sometimes simply expressing disappointment in their company. Every time she learned about unequal pay for women, she made a point to make a phone call or write a letter. Leslie was becoming the Michael Moore of documentaries about women's issues. Rebecca thought Leslie was giving everybody something to think about.

Rebecca hadn't talked to Leslie for a few months, but she would call her as soon as she had a plan. First, she'd check with Angie to find out if she liked the idea of teaming up with other women. Leslie and Angie would make a great team, she thought.

Rebecca took a few notes on the main players she wanted to pitch, finished her espresso and then went to the kitchen to put her cup in the sink. Glancing out the window above the sink, she only saw her distorted reflection. "That's about right," Rebecca said out loud, feeling distorted because of her lingering fear of Roy stalking her.

Rebecca admired how Leslie was able to stand up and confront men and issues that she didn't think were right. Too many times Rebecca hadn't spoken up and had only a few recollections of when she had. One of them was at a Miami football game.

***

She and Jack had arrived early to the game so they decided to grab a couple hotdogs and sit at one of the picnic benches in the food court. When Rebecca overheard some men who were all wearing wedding rings talking about chipping in and getting a friend an escort for his birthday, she was pissed. But Jack was oblivious to what was going on.

One man, loud and obnoxious, talked about his experiences and didn't care who heard him. Rebecca, sitting right next to him, had heard all she could take. "Excuse me. What you are talking about is offensive. There are families and children here who don't want to hear about your shortcomings."

He laughed at her, but the other men heard her loud and clear and their postures and conversation changed. The man who Rebecca had spoken to turned toward her and said, "Well, maybe you shouldn't be eavesdropping in other people's conversations."

"Sir, I'm sitting right next to you, and you are quite loud."

"Stupid bitch," he said under his breath and turned away from her. Their exchange was over.

Jack had finished his hotdog, and Rebecca had lost her appetite so she was ready to go, too. The group of men was also leaving. Jack asked her, "What was that all about? Were you talking to those guys?"

"Yes, honey, I was. One of them called me a stupid bitch."

"What! Where are they?" Jack stuck out his chest, clenched his fists and acted like he was going to go and kick some ass.

Rebecca started laughing. "Very funny, Jack. You timed that perfectly. They're gone," she said still laughing. "But thank you for puffing up for me."

"Let's find them!"

"No, it's fine. I handled it."

"If you see them, point them out. I have a few words for them," he said jokingly, wanting to appear like a tough guy.

Rebecca threw her arms around him and kissed him on the cheek. She felt like the luckiest women in the world to have such a great man. She believed that he knew she could take care of herself; and that alone gave her strength. But then, of course, every other football or basketball game they went to, Jack would say, "Try not to fight with anybody today, okay?"

"Okay, I'll try. But you got my back, right?"

"Of course. Remember last time?" He'd nod his head as if saying, "You don't need to worry about a thing; I'm here for you."

She smiled thinking about another time she spoke up. She was in a public library sitting at a table with a few other adults. At the table next to them sat two teenage girls and a teenage boy. The boy was trying to act like a big shot, swearing and calling some other girls bitches. Rebecca looked over at them and said, "Hey!" looking the boy straight in the eyes. "That's enough!"

He was about to mouth off, but a man sitting at Rebecca's table stopped him with a second and louder, "That's enough!" Rebecca wondered if he would have said something if she hadn't started it.

There again, if women lead, men will follow. Maybe women should take on the role of Morality Police. She giggled.

Rebecca had recently seen in the news the actress Marlee Matlin confessing that she had been sexually abused at age eleven and had suffered domestic abuse. She wrote her name in her notes. Rebecca also wrote down Jane Velez-Mitchell, who had been speaking out about addiction and the war against women, and Mackenzie Phillips, who was speaking out about incest. She wrote down Rihanna, too.

If Angie agreed to team up with other women, Rebecca would pitch full-segment ideas to Primetime, 20/20 and Dateline. She already had plans to pitch Angie alone as an expert on Nancy Grace and Issues with Jane

Velez-Mitchell. Angie could cover everything from missing and exploited children to women who are missing, abducted, raped or murdered.

While working on Angie's plan, Rebecca also started preparing for a trip to New York for a media conference where she would have the opportunity to pitch editors and producers of everything from radio, television, magazines and newspapers. Although there were about three hundred different producers, each PR rep had time to pitch to no more than fifty or so, depending on how quickly you moved around or how quickly you were rejected. Rebecca had been to the conference when she was first starting out on her own, and she was looking forward to attending the event again.

Knowing her subject matter was always a tough sale, Rebecca had to be creative. Her first trip to New York had exposed her lack of experience and naivety. Most wanted funny, happy, uplifting stories about how to make money or how to stay young and attractive. Rebecca was rejected repeatedly, but she made great contacts and many new friends. She couldn't wait to get back; she was ready this time, and her focus would be Angie. Because of famous women speaking out about their own experiences with violence, sexual assault and addiction, Rebecca knew she could get her foot in the door. She wrote down a few pitch ideas. She had big plans for Angie.

In her stack of mail was a book called *Grandmother's Way: Lessons in Love and Life for Young Women* from a potential new client. It was cute. She randomly read through some of the pages and loved the simple style of the book. Each page had an insightful one liner:

Don't do drugs.

Keep good friends.

If you break the law, admit it, accept your consequences and learn from the experience.

Hold out for sex. It makes you a stronger, better person.

Keep your personal space organized, clean and safe.

Don't sleep with married men.

Sometimes making a decision is the best decision … so you can move on with your life.

Your family may be your best friends.

Finish school and keep learning.

Tell the truth.
If you drink, make sure you are safe.
Always trust a person's actions more than you trust their words.
Find a job you love so it doesn't feel like work.
Save sex for somebody who respects you.
Be happy if you have one or two close friends.
Follow rules and laws; it builds character.
Enjoy yourself when you're alone.
Listen to your parents; they may not always be right but always listen.
If you fight with a cop, the cop can hurt you.
Find your purpose for being on this earth.

After paging through the book, Rebecca thought it would make a perfect gift for girls and young women. The book covered everything important in a young woman's life. Rebecca turned to her computer to find out more about this author. The author had written one other book called *Profound Things Women Say*, which Rebecca was able to view from the author's website. It had the same style, very simple one-liners:

God is good to me. I have a warm bed at night. (from a homeless woman in a shelter)
He put his arm around me like a grandfather, then he grabbed my tit. (from a woman working at a restaurant)
Friend 1: I can name tons of things you do for him. Tell me three things he does for you.
Friend 2: (Silence)
Friend 1: Come on, just three.
Friend 2: I don't want to talk about this. (two friends talking)
He sent me a dozen red roses but only because we were fighting. He never sends them when we're getting along. (from a woman talking on her cell phone)
They actually gave me the training I needed to do a good job. (from a woman working in an office)
Learn to laugh at yourself. (from a woman going through chemotherapy)

I'm just asking for some help. These are your kids, too. (from a mother to her ex-husband)

The book was thought-provoking, but not as cute or saleable. It was late and Rebecca was tired. She would finish going through her mail in the morning. She and Lily headed for bed.

Tuesday
3:18AM

SHE HAD A restless night. Lily kept barking and Rebecca kept hearing strange noises all night. She didn't know if it was howling coyotes, the thunderstorm or the wind, but the noises and thoughts of work kept her awake. So at three-eighteen, Rebecca got up and went downstairs to make coffee.

At the last step, she slipped and fell, landing hard on the stairs on her back and butt. She had fallen back on her right arm trying to catch herself, so she gently moved her arm and wrist checking to make sure she wasn't seriously hurt. She wasn't.

When she stood up, she realized that she had slipped in water. There was water on the bottom step. Lily couldn't have done it because she was locked in the bedroom with her all night, and she was still in bed. When she put her hand on the railing, she noticed that the railing was slightly wet as well. "What is going on?" she said, turning on lights and looking up, but seeing nothing that appeared to be leaking. She headed to the kitchen to grab some paper towels.

She was happy she hadn't hurt herself. She had fallen hard, but maybe that extra cushion on her rear had come in handy after all. Rubbing her butt, she started the coffee maker, then went back to wipe up the water. When she bent over, the room started spinning. The scent of Polo was strong, the scent of Roy's cologne. She rushed to the alarm to make sure it was set; it was. She ran to the phone to make sure it had the dial tone; it had. "Okay." She held onto the phone as she rushed around checking all the doors and windows; everything was secure. She ran back up the stairs and Lily joined Rebecca as she rushed around checking the other doors and windows. Everything was locked and the alarm was armed. It had to be her imagination, Rebecca thought, and she started to relax.

She poured herself a cup of coffee, and the telephone rang. Rebecca assumed it was Jack, then realized it would be around two-thirty his time, so there was no way he would call her that early. She answered the phone and the line went dead. Rebecca filled with fear and again started thinking about Roy. She rushed to the living room and closed all the blinds. She checked the alarm again to make sure it was set and saw the red light was on. The alarm was armed. She took a few deep breaths then calmed down by reminding herself that people dial wrong numbers sometimes. That's what it was, a wrong number. But she couldn't get over the fact that as soon as she was up with the lights on, the phone rang. Maybe it was a coincidence.

Rebecca sat down on the couch and started to cry. She felt like she was going crazy. The only other time she felt she was insane was when Roy was stalking her. She remembered coming home and finding one of her blinds open. She never opened that blind because she never used that window. Yet she would convince herself that she had opened it or that her cat must have played with the string and somehow opened the blind. Or she would come home to discover that a light was on even though she remembered turning it off before she left for work. She also thought that her journal had been moved around but never in her wildest dreams did she think that somebody would be stalking her or going into her apartment and going through her things. It was easier to believe she was going crazy.

Rebecca was scared. "What can I do? What can I do?" She didn't care anymore if she looked or sounded paranoid. She was going to make that call to Victim Services and Roy's parole officer. She needed some answers. "Okay, when their offices open, I'm calling!" she vowed. Then she decided to see what she could find out on her own, so she headed to her office and Googled "Roy Smythson".

She was hoping she would find information about him counseling other men with anger or obsessive issues or bipolar disorder. She wanted to read an article about Roy Smythson who turned his lemons into lemonade and he was doing very well. Or how Roy Smythson worked on music while behind bars, his talent and story making him the hot new songwriter in demand. Instead, she learned about other Roy Smythsons: Roy Smythson, the sailing champion; Roy Smythson, the teacher. She kept searching. On page four there was a court hearing document.

"This might be something," she said, clicking on it. The document was from before he was sent to prison. She started reading about the program he was offered instead of prison. Suddenly Rebecca felt a lump in her throat. "I wasn't offered a deal. I didn't get a choice as to what was going to happen to me. He attacked me. Didn't he deserve punishment for what he did to me? I still have hearing damage because of what he did to me. I'm scared for life and he was given a deal?" She kept reading, feeling insignificant and angry.

Suddenly, she was elated. There had been a mistake; he didn't go to prison and he was given a deal. She was thrilled about the program he was offered. She had been afraid for no reason because he never went to prison. She wanted to celebrate. "What a relief! It's over! I can stop worrying." She did have mixed feelings about his lack of punishment but, for her own wellbeing, she'd rather he be rehabilitated and safe in society than in prison full of anger and thoughts of revenge.

She kept reading, skipping the words she didn't understand, until she came to: *The appellant Roy Smythson was charged with one count of assault in the fifth degree and one count of burglary in the first degree for forcefully entering his ex-girlfriend's place of residence and physically assaulting her …*

"I was never his girlfriend!" She continued reading about his felony armed robbery and then skipped ahead.

After completing nearly four months of the anger and substance-abuse residential treatment program …

"Anger and substance-abuse program! What? He didn't have a substance-abuse problem …" or did he? Thinking about his behavior, she kept reading.

Appellant was taken into custody by law enforcement due to his disturbing conduct during a morning anger management class. Appellant started making ape noises in front of other students which became gradually deafening until they were piercing shrieks. The staff attempted to quiet appellant but he continued his disruptive behavior. Law enforcement was called. While the police were restraining him his screams turned to a chant, "I'll kill her! I'm going to kill her ..."

"What!"

Appellant was not allowed back into the program, and his parole officer recommended because of the severity of his crimes that he be sent to prison and his probation be revoked.

Rebecca couldn't believe it. This had to be a mistake. Why didn't somebody tell her. She would call Victim Services as soon as she could. She either wanted Roy's parole officer's phone number or she wanted Victim Services to check with his parole officer to make sure he was still checking in. Would he have a parole officer? Or after serving five years is that it, his time was served? She needed answers. She desperately needed to find out what had happened to Roy. This document made Roy sound crazy, really crazy. How could he be such a mess? She almost felt sorry for him.

"Let me think about this ... let me think." Just because that happened, didn't mean that he hadn't straightened out his life. It didn't mean that he was coming after her. It didn't mean anything. That happened over five years ago. She was sure prisoners received counseling while incarcerated. Rebecca thought about Jack's comment about Roy having five years to plan his revenge. Now that terrified her. "Revenge ... Revenge ..." The word sounded strange to her. She couldn't comprehend its meaning. She grabbed her dictionary and looked up revenge: returning injury.

Should she call Jack? She checked the time and decided to wait until after she had spoken with Victim Services. She felt awful. She was sick to her stomach. She wanted it to be a bad dream. She wanted all of it to go away. She felt so overwhelmed that she didn't want to think about it anymore. She called Lily and they trudged back to bed.

She brought both cordless phones upstairs with her, pushed the chair in front of the door and made sure it was locked. She turned on the TV, but the only thing that was on at that time of morning was a Lifetime movie so she started to watch, hoping it would distract her. But most of all she wanted to go back to sleep and wake up from the dream. Both of Rebecca's thumbs rested between her pinky and ring finger. She was terrified. She had a deep foreboding that Roy was out there, watching her.

Rebecca lay there recognizing that she had become one of *those* women, one of those women who lived in fear, always hiding, stifling their lives to escape being found. Her fear was disrupting her life. It wasn't fair that she had to live like that. Roy was winning. How much time had to pass before she could live fully, without fear? Rebecca started to cry. She didn't want to be afraid; she didn't want to live like that anymore. She would take action. Maybe she would get a gun.

For five years, Rebecca could have been free from worrying about Roy. Five years. Nobody cared enough to even tell her that they had caught up with Roy and that he was going to prison for five years. She could have had five years of freedom.

Maybe this is just the way it is for women. Maybe all women at her age start dealing with these types of fears. Most women have had ex-boyfriends, husbands and lovers. Women have dated people who weren't good for them or weren't healthy. Women have dated the bad boys and the drug addicts or alcoholics. Women have dated the bipolars and the depressed. Women have dated the users and abusers. Women have dated the needy, controlling and the jealous types. Women have dated the really nice guys, only to discover later that they are cheaters or have some deep, dirty past or fetish. By Rebecca's age maybe all women carry a burden of fear because of their pasts with men.

6:05 AM

JACK CALLED AND woke Rebecca.

"My night was good, but I didn't get as much done as I had hoped," she yawned. "How was your night?"

"Well, after we talked I turned on the TV, and I think I was asleep by the first commercial."

Rebecca tried to laugh. "You were tired. How did you sleep?"

"Pretty good. How about you?"

"I didn't sleep well. Lily was barking a lot ... You know, neither of us sleeps well when you're not home. Maybe she's a little nervous without you here." What she wanted to say was, "I'm scared without you here. Please come home."

"Well, I'll be home soon. How are the coyotes?"

"They're around. I hear them every night. In fact, I got up around three and now I'm back in bed ... Oh, my God! I forgot to turn off the coffee maker!" She got out of bed, pushed the chair out of the way and headed downstairs. "I'll take you with me."

"Wow, you beat me getting up. What time did you get to bed last night?"

"I'm not even sure."

"Oh, honey, you're not getting enough sleep. I should let you go back to bed."

Rebecca opened all the blinds after turning off the coffee. It was a beautiful morning, still dark with stars high in the sky and the moon shining brightly. The storm had passed. "I'm glad you woke me. I have a lot on my mind, and I want to finish Angie's packet today, then start on the fun part."

"Your Ps."

"That's right," Rebecca smiled.

"Is everything else okay? You sound a little down."

Rebecca started crying but didn't want Jack to know. "No, I'm okay. I just miss you, that's all."

"I miss you, too. Do you want me to come home? You don't sound yourself, Reb."

"No, honey, I'm fine. I guess I just get a little scared sometimes: the burglar, the coyotes."

"Is the alarm set?"

"Of course."

"Then you're safe, honey. Don't worry. And the coyotes won't hurt you. They are more afraid of you than you are of them."

"Oh, I wouldn't go that far." Rebecca laughed and Jack joined in. Rebecca felt better, with Jack making her feel like nothing could or would ever hurt her.

"Honey, maybe you have cabin fever. Maybe you should call a friend and go have lunch, see a movie or go shopping. Maybe you need to get out of the house for a while."

"You know, that's a good idea. You're probably right," she agreed, knowing that she wouldn't be going anywhere, at least not until she finished what she had set out to do.

Before they hung up, Jack told her to call him any time she needed to talk. He said it didn't matter if he was in a meeting, out for lunch or sleeping, he would answer his phone when she called. He also told her that if she needed him home, he would come home. All she had to do was pick up the phone. Jack reassured her without realizing it, and she knew that sometimes Jack liked to be needed by her. It made him feel important. She did need him—she couldn't imagine life without him.

Although Rebecca's sleep had been restless, she was feeling better. It was starting to lighten outside and that made Rebecca feel safer. Rebecca went back upstairs to make the bed and clean up. She started thinking about the self-defense classes she took right after Roy attacked her, she thought about what she already knew and what she had learned. Before she was attacked, Rebecca believed that she would stay and fight, turn anyone who wanted to hurt her into her victim. But after her experience with Roy, she understood the strength of a man who was crazy on adrenaline. She knew that a hit to the head rattled the brain and caused a fuzzy feeling of disbelief. She knew the first thought after the shock was, "I can't believe this is happening to me." She also knew that the only logical thing to do was to get away and find safety. She was no longer naive about her own strength or ability to fight back.

But Rebecca also knew that though a perpetrator may be physically stronger, he was not mentally stronger than a woman. Perpetrators were cowards who were scared, foolish and error prone. Rebecca knew how important it was to keep your cool, watch and wait for him to make a mistake so you can get away.

From the class she learned: If he grabs you by the wrist, always pull away toward his thumb. It is the weakest part of his grip. If he's in front of you choking you, extend your arms up through the space between the two of you, twist with your elbows out and spin back throwing him an elbow to the face. The elbow is one of our hardest surfaces. If he's holding you from behind, you can punch him in the groin, kick out his knee or grab a weapon like a pencil and stab him in the groin. You can also stomp on his foot as close to his leg as possible. This part of the foot is easy to break and it will disable him from chasing after you. If he's coming at you, you can push the palm or heel of your hand in an upward motion to his nose. Or if he is coming toward you, you can grab him by the shirt or shoulders and knee him in the groin as hard as you can. If you're down on your back, don't let him on you. You can kick at him for as long as it takes; he'll wear out before you do. It doesn't matter if your dress is up around your waist or you've lost a shoe, keep kicking at him. If a perpetrator has a knife or gun and you decide to run, run in a zigzag pattern. If you decide to carry mace, don't depend on it alone; mace can fail. Depend on your hands, knees, elbows and mind to get you through—your brain will never fail you.

Learning self-defense was empowering. The classes gave women some defense tools, but more importantly taught women to stand up straight with their eyes wide open. They gave women confidence that a potential perpetrator would see and then usually decide to find a less confident person to victimize.

Rebecca wanted to be more confident, but she had this nagging feeling that Roy would continue to haunt her. It wasn't just revenge she was concerned about; it was that she would spend the rest of her life living in fear. She wanted her life back.

Rebecca went back downstairs to feed Lily. After Lily finished eating, Rebecca cleaned and refilled her water dish, then took her outside. Rebecca quickly ate some yogurt and a granola bar before going to her office. She found the Victim Services phone number and left a message with her questions and concerns. She worked for three hours organizing her office, filling another garbage bag with unneeded papers. She took notes on Angie as she worked and started to have a clearer idea of the direction her PR would take. Rebecca came up with three exciting ideas and emailed Angie to call her when she got a chance.

11:10 AM

AT A LITTLE after eleven, Rebecca ordered pizza from the only place that delivered out that far and continued working in her office. She felt great. She felt strong, and she was certain that she had been making a big deal about nothing. How could Roy even find her? She had moved several times, and she was married. Besides, as crazy as he seemed, she really didn't believe he would want to hurt her. She never felt he wanted to hurt her; he wanted to be with her. It was control that he wanted, and she wanted to believe she could handle him if he ever showed up.

She could drive herself crazy thinking about somebody hurting her or breaking into her home. It could just as easily be the guy about to deliver pizza or the man who came over a few weeks ago to check and service all the door locks. They didn't know him, yet he was in their home and had access to all of their locks. If she was afraid all the time, if she felt she couldn't take care of herself, then she was no longer living. If fear became her life, how could Jack or any person respect her? How could she respect herself? This crazy fear could keep a victim in a constant state of uncertainty. She would never feel confident, secure or positive about her life if she didn't stay strong and work through her fears.

Rebecca heard a hard thud from downstairs. Lily heard it too and started barking, running to the stairway and looking down, but too afraid to investigate. Rebecca grabbed the phone and dialed 9-1-1 but didn't hit the send button. Rebecca went down the first few steps, then leaned over to check that nobody was there ready to grab her ankles. Lily looked at her like she was insane. Nobody was under the stairs, so she hurried down the rest of the way with Lily following. Nothing was out of place. She walked into the gym and nobody was there. When she turned and started walking toward the bar and pool table, she saw two birds on the pavers outside of the large family-room windows.

There was bird poop running down the pane of glass. One, maybe both of the birds had hit the glass. She felt awful. She hated it when that happened. "Damn it!" she said and turned to look at Lily. "Let's just leave them alone. They may be okay. We'll give them some time to shake it off." She turned to head back upstairs but Lily didn't want to go. "What, baby?"

Lily started to walk toward the bar then stopped.

"Come on, baby, I'm going up." She knew Lily wanted to play down-stairs like they had many times, usually after Rebecca had finished working out. Lily walked around the pool table sniffing the floor. Rebecca thought she saw shoeprints in the carpet. She stepped closer to get a better look. Nobody wore their shoes in the house. She knew that there shouldn't be shoeprints in the carpet. She placed her foot next to the print to measure the size while trying to convince herself that it wasn't a footprint at all. Lily continued sniffing the floor, and then suddenly took off running laps around the pool table. Rebecca laughed and started chasing her. Before long there was no trace of the footprints on the carpet, and Rebecca had deliber-ately erased any trace of them from her mind.

With Lily chasing her, she ran upstairs. Rebecca was starving and couldn't wait for the pizza. She decided to take a quick shower before lunch arrived. While in the shower, she thought she heard another thump, and again Lily started barking. Rebecca thought that maybe the pizza delivery guy was already there though that seemed impossible. She stepped out of the shower, grabbed a towel and walked to the bedroom window, wrapping herself in the towel. She saw somebody on her land, but the figure ducked behind the trees.

She felt exposed with only a towel wrapped around her, so she quickly stepped into the closet and slipped into a pair of sweats and a t-shirt. But she still didn't feel covered enough so she threw on a sweatshirt. She looked out the window again, but there were no cars and the pizza wasn't there yet. She looked past the trees to the open hillside. She looked closer to the house and as far to her left and right as she could. Nobody was there. She used to see her neighbor walking his golden retriever through the field, but he never would have ducked out of sight. If he had seen her, he would have waved. She kept watching to see if the person had walked through the trees and would come out on the other side, but nobody appeared.

If she were to call the sheriff's department to have them keep an eye on her home and if she told them her concerns, would they think she was insane? She thought about how it would sound: Somebody left footprints on my carpet; I think somebody spilled Polo on my stairs; I received a hang-up phone call at three in the morning; I thought I saw somebody walking on my property. "Yep. Crazy." She decided not to call. She pictured the police calling Jack and telling him not to leave his wife home alone anymore.

Rebecca's eyes watered, but she didn't want to cry. She was starting to tell herself to stop thinking about Roy in the *what-if* sense and start thinking about *when*. She knew he was coming for her. She wasn't imagining things, she wasn't going crazy and she wasn't going to call her husband or a security company for a bodyguard. She would take care of this. An odd calm came over her.

Rebecca stood motionless, looking outside and feeling certain that this man would get his revenge. She was so alone, out in the country with neighbors too far away to hear her scream. Would she even be able to scream? Nobody would hear Lily bark. How long would it take the police to get to her? Would she get to the phone in time? She wiped away her tears. She was tired of living part-time in denial and part-time in fear. She knew something had to give.

Rebecca grabbed the phone and headed downstairs. The doorbell rang and Rebecca jumped. Lily again started huffing and puffing as she ran to the door. Rebecca grabbed Lily's leash and attached it to Lily so she wouldn't run outside or jump all over the pizza delivery guy. She could see his truck with the logo on the side. She picked up the money she had set on the table by the door and remembered that she forgot to disarm the alarm. She started yelling, "I got it," and she ran to the keypad. "No! I got it!" she yelled as she opened the front door. "Hi."

Lily was whining, wagging her tail and desperately wanting to jump on the pizza man.

"Hi. Cute dog!"

"Yeah, she's our little watchdog."

"Oh," he said, handing her the boxes. "Your total is twenty thirty-seven."

Rebecca handed him twenty-seven dollars and kept looking past him.

He tried to give her back change, but she kept looking for the man who she thought she had seen. "You okay, miss?"

"Oh, I'm sorry. Keep that. Yes, I'm fine. Listen, did you see somebody around here when you drove up the driveway?"

"No," he said and looked behind him in the direction that she was looking. "I didn't."

"Oh, okay, my brother was supposed to join my husband and me for pizza. He lives over there … he usually walks over. I'm sure he'll be here soon."

"Okay, have a good afternoon."

"Okay, thank you. You, too." She looked down the driveway once more, then closed and locked the door, yelling, "Pizza's here!" so the driver would think that she wasn't alone.

Rebecca knew she hadn't been eating much lately. She didn't feel hungry when she wasn't doing a lot. Because she was just lying around reading, she didn't think her body needed much food. But she knew that *when* Roy came for her, she would need the fuel for her body. Rebecca was still trying to think about Roy in the *when*, not *what if*.

She grabbed a breadstick and started eating. Rebecca had never learned to cook or bake, and it had become the joke of both families and their friends.

***

One day Jack and Rebecca went out to eat with Jack's European friends, and they were looking at photos of their new flat in London. Bernadette was explaining the pictures as they went through them when Rebecca saw a picture of the kitchen and said, "That's a really nice kitchen."

Bernadette leaned over to see the picture she was referring to and said, "Rebecca, you're holding it upside down."

Rebecca was embarrassed, but started laughing, and the others joined in.

Jack seemed to get the biggest kick out of it. "That's my Reb."

Rebecca would fantasize about creating delicious meals and then pigging out, or she'd imagine having a live-in personal chef so she could eat anything she wanted without cooking or having to go to a restaurant.

She thought about the time when Jack had really wanted a grilled cheese sandwich but didn't feel like making it. Rebecca had watched him make grilled cheese sandwiches, so she was confident she could make him one. She got out the bread, butter and cheese. She was pleased to do this for him, and she was going to make the best grilled cheese sandwich he had ever had. She buttered the bread slices and placed them in the pan. She opened the cheese and waited a few minutes before adding it. It was not going well. The bread was getting soggy and the cheese wasn't melting, so she turned up the burner and the bread started to burn. Rebecca started to pout. "I can't do this," she hollered to Jack, who was in his office close by.

"I'll come and help," he said as he came to the kitchen. "What happened?" he asked gently.

"I can't even make a grilled cheese sandwich!" Rebecca whined.

Jack walked over to the stove and looked at the burning grilled cheese. He picked up the spatula and put the burnt sandwich on a plate. He turned toward her and said, "Honey, just … tell me what you did. And start with when you took the cheese and butter out of the refrigerator."

Rebecca started to laugh through her tears. "I'm awful. I'm a horrible wife."

"Honey, you can't cook, but you are a wonderful wife," he said. "How about I make us each a grilled cheese sandwich?"

"No," Rebecca said, sulking, "I'll eat the one I made." Rebecca felt like such a fool. She didn't know how she could screw up a grilled cheese sandwich. After taking a few bites of the burnt, soggy sandwich, she agreed to let Jack make her one of his great grilled cheese sandwiches.

∗∗∗

Thinking of this and eating most of the buttery breadsticks, she laughed at her total lack of cooking skills. She took out a slice of pizza and closed the box. Lily started licking her food dish so Rebecca decided to give her a little extra dog food as a treat. Lily hastily ate a couple morsels and started choking reminding Rebecca of another time she regretted not being able to cook.

***

Jack and Rebecca were in a hurry getting ready to go out with friends, and Lily started choking on her dinner. They waited on the couch with Lily trying to decide what to do, hoping Lily would have one good cough and she would be fine. Lily would cough a little then seem fine, then choke a little, then she was fine again. Worried, they decided to take her to the emergency hospital because all the veterinarian offices were closed. By the time they arrived, Lily seemed fine, but they wanted to be sure. The veterinarian was glad they brought Lily in and she checked her over thoroughly. She gave Lily a liquid medication to ease any pain in her throat and requested that Rebecca make chicken and rice for Lily for about a week because it would be much easier on her throat than the hard, dry dog food.

Rebecca was stunned by the doctor's request. Speechless, she stared at the vet.

"Why are you looking at me that way?" The vet asked. Then she turned to look at Jack and back to Rebecca who was still staring.

Rebecca couldn't get the words out, so Jack helped her out. "Let me put it like this. If Rebecca is cooking chicken and rice in that house, it better be me who gets it for dinner, not Lily … Rebecca doesn't cook."

The veterinarian started laughing. "I understand now," she said looking at Rebecca. "You looked dumbstruck."

"I was," Rebecca laughed.

"Don't worry, we have some canned chicken and rice. I'll send you home with enough to get you through the week."

"Oh, thank you," Rebecca said while holding her hands to her heart.

That canned chicken and rice had looked and smelled so good that she was tempted to have a little herself. And Lily loved it. Rebecca felt bad having to go back to the dry dog food the following week, but at least they found some with smaller morsels.

**

Rebecca finished eating and was tired. She thought about going upstairs to watch some TV and maybe have a nap. Instead she decided to go back downstairs to check on the birds. One of the birds was still there. She looked closely and noticed a few feathers sticking out, but the bird looked fine. She hoped it wasn't in pain. She stepped a little closer and suddenly the bird flew away, surprising Rebecca. "Well, that's that," she said to Lily, thankful that the bird was okay.

They went back upstairs to the kitchen to get her Diet Coke. Rebecca suddenly had the urge to rearrange the furniture in their living room. She turned on the stereo and put in an Aaliyah CD. She started dancing around the living room, as she tried to figure out how to change things. She liked the way their living room was arranged but hated a bookcase that stood against a wall at the bottom of the stairs.

The bookcase was light oak with glass shelves. She tried to figure out where she could move it, she wished she could put it in Jack's office because he loved it, but she didn't think there was room. She wanted to set it out in the garage and use it for storage, but Jack would not be happy if he came home and found his bookcase in the garage with paint cans on it. Plus, she had no idea where she'd put the knickknacks, glass sculptures and books that sat there collecting dust. Not only was the bookcase out of place, but she didn't like the glass pieces it contained: a wolf, which too closely resembled a coyote, and a bear. They were beautiful, she had to admit, but they weren't her taste. Just because they lived in the country didn't mean their home had to resemble a cabin.

Jack hated her moving things around. Rebecca remembered the look on his face every time he came home to find everything changed. His disapproving look didn't last long because there was one thing that made it all okay—he loved her. And when she was happy and proud of her decorating, he was happy and proud, too. But they both knew her need to rearrange was a distraction from work, and at the moment she felt the need for a distraction very much.

The doorbell rang and alarmed Rebecca. She looked out the windows on the sides of the front doors and recognized one of her other neighbors and his sons who lived about a mile away. She remembered Jack telling her that Ron and his wife were getting a divorce, and Ron had bought each of his boys a puppy as a way to compensate for the divorce.

"Hold on," she yelled and hit the off button on the stereo, then ran to turn off the alarm. She opened the door and Lily slipped out. She jumped up and licked one of the little boys. He giggled and pet Lily on the head.

"Sorry to bother you, Rebecca. We're hoping you've seen our two golden lab puppies. They've been missing since some time last night."

Rebecca hoped her concern about the coyotes didn't show as she said, "No, I haven't seen them." She grabbed Lily's harness and pulled her into the house. "Come on, Lily."

"I'm hoping one of the neighbors pulled them inside, you know, because of the coyotes. You're our first stop."

"Oh, I'm sure somebody has your puppies. I'm sure you'll find them." She smiled at the boys.

"Yeah, me too." He put his hand on his son's shoulder. "Well, we better keep looking."

"Okay. Well, good luck and I'll call you if I see anything."

"I appreciate it," Ron said, and they turned and walked back to their car.

As Rebecca watched them drive down the driveway, she decided to skip rearranging the living room and get back to work. She started thinking about her behavior when the pizza arrived. She knew that her performance was that of a woman, never a man. She had ordered enough pizza for four so the delivery man would believe that she wasn't alone. She had acted as though she was talking to others in the house and was expecting more people soon. Rebecca felt her eyes burn and hated how tortured she'd become. She was in a cage, feeling unsafe and vulnerable.

She had heard all the advice that kept women caged: Don't go out alone at night. Don't drink. Carry your keys between your fingers. Park under street lights if you have to go out at night. Carry mace. Don't dress sexily. Don't go jogging at night or alone. Take self-defense classes. Don't sound like you live alone on your answering machine.

Rebecca couldn't believe that in this wonderful country and modern world we still had rape. She knew that the responsibility of rape still focused on the victim and not the predator, which often kept the women from reporting it. And the meaning of rape had become blurred. She learned from Angie's work that many boys and girls didn't know exactly what rape was. Many young people believed that if it isn't a violent attack by a stranger, it isn't rape. Some young people also believed that in certain situations a male had the right to have sex with a female whether she wanted to or not.

Rebecca remembered an article about how many of the strong, courageous military women who were victims of rape did not report it because they thought it was an expected part of military service for women.

Rebecca knew that most crimes were committed because perpetrators believed they could get away with it. They preyed on the weak and the vulnerable, believing that the weak and vulnerable were women and children. If women started killing the perpetrators who attempted or succeeded in hurting them or their children, would these crimes decline? But Rebecca had never heard of a potential victim killing her perpetrator.

She took a deep breath and decided it was time to take Lily out, but because of the cold and because Rebecca felt jumpy, they stayed close to the house. Lily looked up toward the hill and started barking. Rebecca heard something and looked for movement on the hill. About eight deer were grazing there behind a few trees. "Oh, Lily, they're beautiful." Lily stopped barking, watched for a while, then squatted to go potty.

Rebecca watched the deer until they moved deeper into the trees. She and Lily strolled to the side of the house and Lily ran to something she saw lying on the grass. As Rebecca got closer, she cried out and held Lily back. It was a leg from their jackrabbit, Fred, and it was fresh. Rebecca picked up Lily, looked around and hurried around the house and back inside. She locked the door, set the alarm and headed straight upstairs to the safe room.

Sad and afraid, Rebecca was starting to get angry. She turned on the TV and the news was on. She got into bed and pulled the covers up but couldn't get warm. She tried to cuddle with Lily, but Lily was more interested in one of her chew toys. Rebecca got up, turned up the heat and crawled back into bed. After about 15 minutes, she decided to run a hot bath. She checked the alarm and saw it was armed. She walked over and checked the door; it was locked. She walked through their bedroom, into the closet and into the bathroom to make sure no one was there. Her head felt stuffy, so she sniffed to see if she could breathe normally through her nose. She couldn't. "Oh, please, no. I can't have a cold." She knew she should go back to bed, but she didn't think she'd be able to sleep until she was warm.

When the tub was half full, she lowered herself into the hot water. "Ah," she sighed, knowing she'd soon feel better and hoping the steam would open her sinuses.

When Jack shared the tub with her, he wanted the jets on. Again, their differences were obvious: Rebecca liked a quiet soak, and he liked a noisy, bubbling tub. Even though she missed Jack and loved everything about him, even the things that bugged her, at this moment she was thankful to have the quiet, relaxing soak alone. Rebecca thought about how she and Jack had ended up together.

***

The evening after Jack showed up with the heart-shaped candle, he called and asked for another date. He was in Las Vegas for a conference and would like her to fly to Vegas on Friday after work for a weekend date. Other than cleaning her apartment, Rebecca had no plans that weekend, so she said yes. After she hung up, she went online to look for a cheap flight and a hotel room on the strip. Twenty minutes later, she buzzed up a courier with a package from Jack. The package contained a plane ticket, a hotel reservation and a note from Jack, saying, "I'll pick you up at the airport Friday night."

The next day Rebecca took her ticket and note to work to show her friends.

"Rebecca, this is a first-class ticket."

"No, it isn't," she said, snatching the ticket away from Carol. "How do you know?" She pointed at the ticket. "See this." Rebecca looked. "First-class. Who is this Jack and how did you meet?"

"Why would he send me a first-class ticket? Why would he send me a ticket at all?"

"I know why …" Carol raised her eyebrows and smiled.

"Well, I can't go then!"

"Come on. Separate rooms, right? I'm just kidding. Go. Have fun. Live a little." Carol grabbed the ticket. "If you don't, I will."

"You're married."

"Not for him, you dork. I love Vegas. I love the slots." She handed Rebecca the ticket. "Listen, you have a credit card right?"

"Yes."

"Well, go have fun. If anything weird happens, grab a cab, get on a plane and fly home. What's the problem?"

"You're right. There's no problem. I'm going."

Jack and another man met Rebecca at the baggage claim, and the man picked up her bag from the carousel. Jack grabbed Rebecca's hand and followed the man out to a black limousine. Rebecca was very nervous. She didn't even know Jack, so what was she doing?

He told Rebecca that he had reservations for dinner, but they would go to the hotel first so she could freshen up. "I know I sent you a reservation for your own room but …"

Oh, no. Rebecca thought.

"We actually have a suite with two bedrooms, I hope that's okay?"

"Yes, that's okay." And then Rebecca thought, we'll see. She felt safe with her escape plan in place.

They entered the hotel through a different door than other guests, greeted with a glass of champagne and then escorted to their room. Since Jack had been there for a couple of days, all the special treatment was for Rebecca's benefit. Fresh flowers and original art works lined the halls on their way to their room. The man accompanying them opened a large door and said, "Enjoy your stay."

Eager to get to her room, Rebecca stood there waiting for somebody to show them to their suite. Jack tipped the man, then gave Rebecca a quick kiss. "I'm glad you're here ... Oh, your bag will be here in a minute. Your bedroom is over here," he said walking down the beautiful wide hall. Bewildered, Rebecca realized they were already in their suite. Her bedroom had a king bed with luxurious white linens, a desk with a computer, an armoire with a TV inside and a sitting room with a couch and two chairs. The bathroom was luxurious with a separate room for the toilet, bidet and sink. There was a huge shower to the left and a soaking tub to the right with a TV mounted inside the wall encased in glass.

The butler unpacked Rebecca's bag for her and took some of her clothes to have them pressed. The lack of privacy upset Rebecca a little, but she decided not to let it bother her. She freshened up, and she and Jack went out to dinner.

That night after dinner, wearing only a t-shirt and panties, Rebecca walked into his bedroom to thank him and to say good night. He was lying in bed wearing red plaid pajamas. She got into bed with him under the covers. They faced each other and talked until they were both tired. Jack leaned in and gave Rebecca a kiss on her lips then rolled over. He didn't say she was welcome to stay in his bed, or that she had to leave.

Rebecca lay there looking at his back, confused, feeling a bit rejected and wanting to laugh. She gently got out of bed and walked into the living room. She sat down at the piano but didn't touch the keys. She wanted to soak it all in. After a few minutes, she stood and walked over to the large dining room table. She leaned over to smell the fresh flower centerpiece. She walked back into the living room and sat on the couch. Next to the couch was a table with more fresh flowers and a monitor to control the room's many features. Rebecca touched the screen, then touched All Lights Off. The lights slowly dimmed to complete darkness, with only the monitor glowing. She touched Open All Drapes and all the drapes opened. She stood up and walked to the windows. She didn't know they had a balcony. She opened the doors and stepped outside. It was beautiful with Las Vegas lights filling the sky. It was warm, and there were flowers and trees on their lanai. She lay down on a chaise, and wanted to wake up Jack so he could see how beautiful it was. But she figured he had seen it all before.

Rebecca fantasized that she was married to Jack and that this was her life. Everything around her was beautiful and elegant. She didn't have a care in the world. Anything she wanted was a phone call away. The fantasy was fun, but she knew that it wouldn't make her happy because she wanted to be successful in her own life. Rebecca thought about her career. She didn't want to continue working for Response PR as their secretary or helper. Rebecca had already helped create hugely successful campaigns for some of Response PR's clients. She had openly shared her ideas in hopes of being promoted, but she was feeling less and less appreciated. Rebecca had also given up some of her media contacts that she had made while working for Ed. Feeling more confident of her ability to succeed on her own in the public relations field, Rebecca wanted her own clients.

She thought about how she had kept progressing in her life. Except for the mess with Roy, Rebecca was really happy, and she was energized about her future. She believed she was ready to either ask for a promotion or branch out on her own. Her mom had a lot of connections and offered her assistance many times, but Rebecca hoped she could do it on her own.

When Rebecca wasn't at work, she was home working to create a business plan for her own PR firm. She had a detailed design created for a website. She had her letterhead and business cards designed in lavender and brown. And she had a direction helping women—but she didn't have a name or logo yet.

Rebecca stood up and looked out over the courtyard of The Mansion. She could see a beautiful swimming pool with a fountain. There were lemon trees and flowers scenting the night air. She breathed in deeply and exhaled slowly. She thought about how she kept moving forward in her life, learning and growing every day. There it was, she knew the name of her future PR firm—Women Going Forward. "Women Going Forward," she said out loud. She liked the way it sounded. She would create a community of women who fight for change in their lives and the lives of all women. She sat back down on the chaise and stretched out. "Women Going Forward," she murmured closing her eyes and visualizing her success. She fell asleep outside on the balcony dreaming about her future business.

Jack woke her early the next morning with coffee and fresh Krispy Kreme donuts. He had a little gift for her, a small turquoise box from Tiffany's. She couldn't believe it. "*Breakfast at Tiffany's* is my favorite book!"

Jack smiled. "Open it."

Inside was a little silver ring with a raindrop attached. Rebecca loved it. "Thank you so much," she said, trying not to cry. She reached for him and gave him a hug.

"You're welcome."

Just then, they looked at each other in shock. "I felt a raindrop."

"So did I, but it doesn't rain in Vegas," Jack said as the downpour started. They stayed outside in the rain holding hands. Rebecca knew the ring and the downpour were a sign of good things to come.

***

Rebecca twisted her ring while she sat in the bath deep in memories of that Vegas trip with Jack. She was glad they got to know each other better before making love. They waited almost eight months and the memory of that first night flooded over her.

***

They were at a dinner party with Jack's friends and co-workers. Jack put his hand on her leg, and she could feel the intense heat and passion in his touch. He wanted her and made no secret of it. He moved his hand up on her thigh and his strong hands and fingers caressed her inner thigh, making her catch her breath and feel lightheaded. Her body was reacting in ways she never thought possible. She wanted him so badly that if he kept touching her with his hand that way, they would be making love in the bathroom in a few minutes.

After moving his hand away, Rebecca stood up and walked across the room. She grabbed a bottle of water from the table and turned to look at Jack. He had his eyes on her, but kept talking to his coworker. Rebecca watched his lips move as he spoke. She desperately wanted to kiss him and feel his body against hers. She loved him, and she knew he loved her too.

At her place after the dinner party, Rebecca had the sexiest, most stimulating conversation of her life. Jack turned her on with his words, his eyes and his touch. He sat across from her with his hands on her knees. He told her that he wanted her. "I've never wanted anybody as much as I want you right now," he said softly. His words were strong and sincere.

Trembling with anticipation, Rebecca had never felt sexier, more beautiful or more desired.

"I don't want to rush you, but I want you to know how much I love you, and I'm hoping we can take this relationship to the next level."

Rebecca gently nodded her head.

Jack knelt on the floor between her legs and began kissing her. Holding her face in his hands, his hands gently slid down across her breasts and rested on her hips. Rebecca wrapped her arms around his shoulders and as they stood up, he lifted her and carried her to the bedroom. Jack and Rebecca made love that night, and it was beautiful.

The next morning while lying in bed together, Jack reached over to his jacket on the floor and pulled out another turquoise box from Tiffany's. Jack proposed to Rebecca.

And Rebecca began her perfect life. Until she received that letter in the mail stating that the state had caught up with Roy and they needed her in court. After listening to her 9-1-1 call, she decided to follow through, arriving at the courthouse only to learn that Roy had run again and he was still out there roaming the streets. Rebecca didn't go into much detail when explaining the situation to Jack. Her life before had been so different; she didn't want to think about it or talk about it. She just wanted to let it go and move forward with her perfect life with Jack.

Jack and Rebecca waited only a few months before going to Las Vegas to get married. They chose Vegas for two reasons: it was convenient to fly people into, and their first real date was in Las Vegas. They had a small, elegant ceremony in The Mansion with twenty of their family and closest friends. Like in the fairytales, Rebecca wore a beautiful white wedding dress and Jack, a black tuxedo. Rebecca walked herself down the aisle, and Jack walked up the aisle to meet her half-way—the perfect metaphor for their perfect marriage.

***

Rebecca got out of the tub, dried off and got into bed. Warm under the covers, she was grateful for her life so she decided to pray. Rebecca rarely prayed when things were bad. She liked to pray when her life was good. She wanted to give thanks for her blessings. She hadn't prayed for a long time, but a few nights before Jack left town, she had remembered her special childhood prayer and ritual.

***

Rebecca was in bed lying next to Jack when she could tell that Lily was antsy. She decided to take her outside in case she had to go potty. Rebecca sat up and looked at the clock. It was a little after one in the morning.

Jack asked, "Do you want me to take her?"

"No, honey, that's okay. I'll take her." Rebecca yawned as she walked down the hall to the stairs. She heard Lily jump off the bed. At the door, Rebecca attached Lily's leash and they headed outside. After Lily peed they went back inside and crawled back into bed. Jack wrapped himself around Rebecca, his warm breath on her shoulder. She felt blessed. Rebecca clasped her hands in prayer. Her hands felt thin compared to Jack's. She was more used to holding Jack's hand than her own. Her own hands felt awkward; it had been too long.

She used to pray every night before bed, a ritual that meant everything to her. Prayer kept her on track. She didn't remember when she started her ritual, but she knew she was very young. After saying the, "Now I lay me down to sleep ..." prayer, she would pray for everybody she knew and loved. She also prayed for anybody she felt needed a little extra prayer, people she heard about, strangers. But it was the next little piece of her prayer ritual that she missed the most. Rebecca would kiss her folded hands, then use her hands as healers and gently glide her hands over her body not touching, just hovering over. She blessed herself and her body. She started at her face, going down the front, then up the back. Once she was finished, she would imagine her body as a pebble in a pond. She would visualize the healing vibration from her body going out and reaching the world. It started with everybody in her house. When she was little it went out to her dad and sister, but on this night the loving energy went to Jack and Lily, then out to their neighbors, the town, the state, over every state, through the ocean, to other countries, the world and into the universe. Once her ritual was done, she slept well.

***

Rebecca decided to do her childhood ritual while snuggled in with Lily. She said her prayer in her mind, and prayed for everybody she knew and loved. She prayed for Melvin and his new tires. She prayed for Angie and Leslie and Christy. She even prayed for Roy. She kissed her hands and covered her body with healing power. Next she imagined this power penetrating Lily, the neighbors, all the way throughout the universe. She drifted off to sleep, content and happy.

5:05 PM

REBECCA WOKE FROM her nap thirsty for some cold water. She had turned the heat up too high in the bedroom, but she had had a great rest and she felt better; she could breathe through her nose again. She wasn't sick.

She called to Lily, and she turned the alarm off. She attached Lily's leash and they stepped outside heading toward a hill where Lily seemed to like doing her business. It was still light out, but the sun was going down and the air was chilly. At least it wasn't raining. Lily sniffed around and Rebecca yawned. Rebecca thought she heard something, but Lily didn't seem concerned. Rebecca looked up toward the hills expecting to see deer, but there was nothing there. Finally, Lily peed but she kept sniffing around so Rebecca figured she had to poop as well.

Again, Rebecca thought she heard a sound. Nervous, she pulled Lily's leash, and they headed down the small hill away from the trees toward the front door. Stepping off the grass and onto the driveway, Rebecca heard another sound—there stood a coyote only thirty feet from them.

Rebecca yelled, "Get outta here!" and flapped her arms.

The coyote stared at her. He didn't run; he wasn't afraid. Lily didn't see the coyote and didn't know what was going on. Rebecca picked up Lily and walked backward toward the front door, yelling, "Get! Get out!" The coyote stood still, watching them. When they were close to the front door, Rebecca screamed and lunged at the coyote. But it still didn't move.

Rebecca hurried Lily into the house. Only when Lily was inside did the coyote head back up toward the trees on the hill. Rebecca kept repeating, "Coyotes are afraid of humans. They won't hurt you. They are afraid of you." Wanting to make sure they were afraid of her, she grabbed a handful of rocks and walked toward where the coyote had been standing. The closer Rebecca got to the spot, the more afraid she became. If the coyote was rabid, it would attack her. And she didn't have her phone with her. She wasn't that big next to that coyote, so she turned around and headed back inside.

Rebecca went straight to the phone, then reset the alarm system. She dialed Jack's cell. "Hi honey!" he answered.

"Jack, a coyote was standing on that rock by our house while I was outside with Lily!"

"Are you kidding me?"

"No!"

"Are you both okay?"

"Yes, but I'm pissed! That coyote wasn't scared of me ... at all!"

"What do you mean?"

"I yelled, flapped my arms and even charged at it. It didn't move."

"Oh, my God. Maybe it was rabid."

"That's what I was thinking. I've seen them run off before ... I've scared them off myself. This one wasn't afraid."

Jack was silent.

"Hello?"

"... Yeah ... I'm sorry. I'm thinking."

Rebecca waited.

"Okay, if you see the coyote again I want you to call the sheriff and get the number of who to call about problem animals. In the meantime, you two stay close to the front door, okay?"

Rebecca had already planned on calling the sheriff to get that phone number. Glad they were on the same page, she also already knew she and Lily would be staying by the front door. "Okay."

"God, Rebecca, that's awful. What are we going to do about those coyotes?"

"I don't know. That stupid coyote got Fred too!"

"How do you know?"

"Because his leg was lying in our yard."

"Oh, God, Rebecca, I'm going to worry about you and Lily now until I get home. Promise me you won't go far from the door, even during the day."

"I won't."

"Rebecca!"

"I won't! I'm scared of them, but I'm getting pissed. I want to go and hunt it down ..." she sighed loudly. "Don't worry about me, I'm tough."

"I know you are. I love you and be careful."

"I love you, too, and I will."

Rebecca hung up the phone and could hear the wind again. She looked out the kitchen window and watched the trees bending in the gusts. She looked for coyotes but didn't see any. That coyote had made her so angry that, for the first time, she wished she had had a gun. She would have used it.

Wednesday
5:38 AM

THE SECURITY ALARM started wailing. Rebecca threw off the covers, jumped out of bed and ran down the hall to the stairs. By the time she reached the steps, she was awake enough to realize she was scared and didn't know what to do. She wasn't following her plan. She turned on the hall light, then the downstairs light and peered over the railing overlooking the living room but saw nothing. The alarm was piercing so she ran back to the bedroom to turn it off. She grabbed the phone waiting for it to ring. With the phone in hand, she headed downstairs. About halfway down the stairs, she stopped and leaned over the railing to get a better look. She listened. Lily, totally unconcerned, was still in bed. Rebecca listened hard, trying to make sense of the alarm going off. She heard her own breathing and thought she could hear her own heartbeat.

Why hadn't their security service called? She continued down the stairs and, when she got to the kitchen, she decided to call them herself. There was no dial tone. Holding the phone, she ran to the other phone in the living room. She picked it up and pressed talk. The line was dead. "Oh, my God." Still holding the phone she ran back upstairs and back into the bedroom, locking the door behind her. She sat on the bed shivering with fear and tried to think it through. "Okay, if the power went out, the alarm could have gone off and that might explain the phones, but the power is on now; the phones should work. Okay, maybe I should go back downstairs and check the wall phone in the kitchen." She stood at the door, took a deep breath and listened intently to hear if somebody was in the house. She heard nothing but Lily's snoring and her own breathing. She turned the doorknob and raced down the stairs toward the kitchen. She quickly ran into the kitchen, grabbed a knife from the rack as she passed and grabbed the phone on the wall. There was a dial tone. She pulled the phone to the garage door to get the security company's phone number and dialed.

"My alarm went off and nobody came and you never called. I'm alone and I'm scared."

The operator gently told her to calm down. "Let me check. Okay here it is. No, we have no record of activity there."

"That's impossible!"

"You're calling from your home phone, right? Well, give me your address."

"Number 15 Mountain Hill."

"Yes, that's what we have, and I see no activity at that address.

"Will you please check your system? How could the alarm go off, and you have no record? This doesn't make sense!"

"Honey, if you think somebody broke in, please hang up and call 9-1-1 or I can dispatch for you."

"No. I don't know. It's a big house."

"Have you had any power outages recently? Or construction, or window washers can sometimes trip the system for no reason."

"No we haven't … You know, I'm sorry. I'm sure it's just some freak thing. I'm sorry to have bothered you."

Rebecca hung up the phone and stopped herself from crying. Lily had found her way downstairs and was jumping against Rebecca's legs wanting to comfort her. Rebecca set the knife on the counter and sat down on the floor. She let Lily lie on her lap. She felt like she was going crazy. Did the alarm really go off at all? She threw her head back and bumped the wall.

The phone rang and startled Rebecca. She looked at the clock on the microwave. It was almost six. She looked at the restricted number on the caller ID and knew that it would be another hang up. She answered it certain that it wouldn't be Jack and that it would be the same person as before, Roy.

It was Jack.

"Honey, it's five o'clock your time."

"I know but it's really six for me. I've already ordered my coffee. Should be here any time. How was your night? Did you see any more coyotes?" Jack asked.

"No, we haven't been outside since I talked to you last."

"Have you heard any more from the neighbor about the burglar yet?"

"No, nothing new. I'm sure it had something to do with their kids or … I mean who burglarizes a home and cuts down a tree? Oh, and then Ron and his boys stopped by. They were missing their two yellow lab puppies. I'm afraid that the coyote's got them …"

"Isn't that strange. We never seemed to worry about anything when we lived in the city?"

"I know, it's true. But I like it out here. We're fine, Jack. Everything will be fine."

"I just love you, and I want you to be safe and happy."

"I love you, too. And I am happy. I've never been happier."

"I can't wait to get home and crawl into bed with you. I miss you."

"I miss you, too. But I'm fine."

"Okay, call me if you need anything … Anything, Reb."

Rebecca hung up the phone. She took a deep breath and tried to relax. She couldn't. She decided to call her mom because it wasn't that early in New York. "Hi, Ruth. It's Rebecca."

"Hi, Rebecca. How are you?"

"Well, to be honest, I'm not doing that well. I feel like I'm going crazy. Remember I told you all about Roy and the trouble I had. Well, he's been released from prison and I'm home alone and I'm just … nervous."

"Oh, yes, I remember."

"I know you don't like to hear about it, and you think I'm making a big deal out of nothing, but I guess … I just wish I knew that he wouldn't bother me." She paused. "Strange things keep happening, and I get the feeling that he's watching me."

"Well, I'll tell you, Rebecca, he won't bother you. Too much time has passed. He doesn't care one bit about where you are and what you're doing. Plus, he probably feels sorry for everything and knows the best thing to do is to leave you alone. Really, Rebecca, you have to let this go. It will destroy you if you always live with this hanging over you, being afraid."

Rebecca took a deep breath. "Thank you, Ruth, I needed that. I wish I didn't get scared, but I do."

"Rebecca, I understand, it's fresh. Time will pass, nothing will happen and you will start to forget about it."

"You're right."

"How is work going? You know, diving into work always helps me feel better."

Rebecca smiled. She knew Ruth well. "Yes, I have some work to do."

"Well, good. You get back to work and you'll forget all about this Ray guy."

Rebecca didn't correct her. "I'll do just that. Thanks, Ruth."

Rebecca hung up the phone, then took Lily outside. There was nothing out of the ordinary, but she stayed close to the front door and she didn't see a coyote. Lily did her business quickly and they ran back inside. After resetting the alarm, Rebecca followed her mom's advice and got back to work.

In Angie's packet, Rebecca found a cute article from a men's health magazine about Angie and "The Top Seven Reasons Men Shouldn't Be Afraid of the Feminist":

- *It's the new millennium and we're not going anywhere.*
- *We are still feminine and love being women.*
- *If you fall in love with a feminist you'll learn to stand for something.*
- *If you're bad in bed we'll tell you, then we'll teach you.*
- *You just might be a feminist yourself.*
- *If we smell fear on you, we're more likely to attack.*
- *The most important reason to not be afraid of the feminist is that men and women are more alike than different. Men and women want the same things: both want to feel important, appreciated and valued, both want to love and be loved.*

Rebecca remembered her conversation with a man at Book Expo America in Chicago a couple years ago. He expressed his disapproval of feminism after learning that Rebecca was a feminist. Instead of walking away, she decided to stay and listen and was surprised to learn that, in her opinion, he was also a feminist. She was even more surprised when he said, "I can't believe you're a feminist, you're so nice."

Rebecca had been a feminist her entire life. She had her mom and dad to thank for that, not to mention her friends. Rebecca was amazed to learn that not only men, but also women were confused about what it meant to be a feminist. A feminist believes that men and women are equal. Different, sure, but equal. That's it. After Rebecca explained the meaning to most people they realized that they, too, were feminists.

This feminist article was one of the most enjoyable in Angie's packet. She giggled about number four, having known far too many women who faked orgasms and were, therefore, clearly not feminists. Rebecca's orgasm was just as important as anybody else's who was in the room.

Suddenly, Rebecca was up on her feet, listening intently to a scraping sound coming from upstairs. Lily was on the floor by the fireplace and seemed to hear it too. This time Rebecca didn't grab the phone on her way to the stairs because she was pretty sure she knew what it was. She listened as she quietly stepped up each step with Lily following. She wished Lily wasn't so clumsy and noisy. After they passed through the bedroom doorway, Rebecca quickly ran to the deck off the master bedroom and threw opened the door yelling, "Get out of here!"

The alarm started blaring and three huge ravens flew off the roof. Rebecca had forgotten about the alarm. She slammed the door and ran to the bedroom keypad to turn it off. The phone rang shortly after. Once she assured the security company that she was fine and gave them the pass code, she plopped down on the bed. "Ugh! If it's not one thing troubling me, it's something else."

12:50 PM

REBECCA WAITED FOR the return phone call from Victim Services. She assumed that they were taking their time doing some of their own checking and, because they hadn't rushed to call her back, Rebecca believed she had nothing to worry about.

She spent a couple hours in her office, making phone calls and getting ready for her upcoming trip to New York for the PR convention. Her office was now clean and organized, almost paperless. She was excited about this new way of working. She wasn't sure how well she would be able to keep it up because sometimes she needed hard copy in her hands, but she was looking forward to traveling lighter.

Rebecca had finished reading through Angie's packet. She had high hopes that she could get Angie to be a regular commentator on a mainstream news outlet as an expert on violence against women and children. She had received a few emails back from producers who were interested. And she would like to connect Angie with other women who were working to improve the lives of women and children. Rebecca had drafted two press releases, but she needed to talk to Angie before she could go any further and she couldn't wait to do that.

Rebecca felt great. Everything she had wanted to accomplish during Jack's trip, she'd accomplished. She decided it was time to celebrate with a workout, a soak in the hot tub and a steam. She changed her clothes and headed downstairs to the gym.

After her vigorous workout, Rebecca soaked in the hot tub. She started the jets and relaxed as the water pulsated against her muscles. She thought about getting out a bottle of wine, but decided to watch a movie instead. Rebecca loved to reward herself when she achieved her goals, and there were a couple of movies on pay-per-view that she wanted to see. She really didn't want to drink alone anymore. She didn't want to wonder if she were trying to escape something. She would rather deal with her feelings: good or bad, loneliness or euphoria. But she would have a glass of wine with Jack or friends.

Soaking in the hot tub, she looked out at the blue sky and mountains. She hadn't seen the sky that blue since Jack surprised her for her birthday in Orlando.

***

Jack had to work on her birthday, but told her he would meet her at their cabana at the hotel pool for lunch. He brought a few friends from work to join them. There was some whispering going on and Rebecca knew he was up to something, but she never could have guessed. A beautiful birthday cake for dessert was brought out by the staff singing "Happy Birthday."

What a wonderful surprise, she thought. But that wasn't all.

Jack had hired a pilot to write "I Love You Reb" across the sky with his airplane. Rebecca cried and held onto Jack tightly while the plane created the letters. Jack's friends took photos and video of the event. Later, Jack bought her a gorgeous blue sweater set that was the same color as the sky that day, making it a most memorable birthday. As much as Rebecca appreciated his gifts and thoughtfulness on her birthday, Jack was Rebecca's favorite gift every day of every year.

***

Rebecca decided to skip the steam and headed upstairs to shower.

Wrapped in a towel, she stepped into her closet and saw that blue sweater set. She couldn't wait for Jack to get home. She slipped into her pajamas and intended to lounge around the rest of the day. As she went down the stairs, she glanced out the window and saw a coyote in the distance on a hill far from their yard. She watched it until it disappeared into the trees. Rebecca needed to take Lily outside and dreaded it. But it had to be done, so she turned off the alarm and walked to the front door where Lily was waiting.

Rebecca stayed close to the house. Hypersensitive about the coyotes, she walked Lily around as much as she could in the small area by the front door. But Lily wanted to go for a walk, so Rebecca grabbed a few rocks and walked a little farther from the house. Lily sniffed the grass and Rebecca waited.

"Come on, Lily."

Lily stopped everything and looked right at Rebecca.

Rebecca laughed. "Yes, I'm talking about you. Hurry up."

Lily continued sniffing around.

Rebecca had to go to the bathroom herself, so she squatted. When finished, she pulled her pajama bottoms back up and tied the string snuggly around her waist. Lily walked over and sniffed where Rebecca had gone, then squatted and peed right on top of Rebecca's. "My word. If I had known it could be that easy, I would have peed for you before." Rebecca shook her head. "So, you're going to mark on top of my marking? You think this is your territory?" Rebecca picked up Lily. "I sure love you. Let's go watch a movie."

Once inside with the alarm back on, she got comfortable on the couch and covered up with the throw. She turned on "American Justice" on A&E. Lily snuggled in next to her, and they both fell asleep.

About an hour later Rebecca woke up and started flipping through the channels. The movie, *A Perfect Murder*, was just getting ready to start on HBO, so she decided to skip pay-per-view. Rebecca slipped out from under the blanket trying not to wake Lily. She got a bag of microwave popcorn and poured herself a big glass of milk while waiting for the popcorn to finish popping. Then she settled in with Lily to watch the movie.

Rebecca had a great night. She didn't work at all. She snacked, watched movies and peed outside again with Lily before they headed to bed for the night.

Thursday
2:18 AM

REBECCA WOKE TO a dark figure hovering over her.

"Jack!" She tried to sit up but was held down.

"It's not Jack."

Rebecca froze. She knew that voice—it was Roy. "Jack will be home any minute."

"Jack is out of town," he said and leaned over to turn on the light. He was sitting next to her on the edge of the bed.

His dark hair was gone; his head was shaved bald.

Rebecca was scared but strangely at ease. Maybe he just wanted to talk, she thought.

"How did you get in here? The alarm ..."

"You're foolish," he interrupted. "But you did well for yourself," he said as he looked around. "It's so funny ... you thought you were so safe setting your alarm all the time." He laughed. "I busted one of your door locks even before your prince left town. Every time you turned off your alarm, I had easy access. And once I was in, your old system was easy to jack up. Get it? Jack ... up? You should have updated your system ..." He laughed. "Well, it probably wouldn't have done any good. I still would have found a way ... Your phones are down, too, so don't even think about ..."

"Why are you here? What do you want?"

"I haven't decided yet. But, I wanted to see you again."

"Did you cut ..."

"… cut down your neighbor's tree? Yes."

"You've been in this house, haven't you?"

"Almost daily."

Without warning, Roy raised his arm and powerfully struck her across the left side of her face.

The pain was immediate. Her eye quickly swelled up almost to the point of being closed. Panic flooded her. Was this the end of her life? Tonight would it all end? She didn't want to die. She had to fight. More than anything she wanted to hit him back, but she knew it would be a mistake. She had to think. "Where's Lily?"

"Your dog? I locked him up."

"Lily!" She yelled in panic, then heard Lily scratching at a door and crying. "Outside?"

"Your office." Rebecca felt relieved just hearing her. As Rebecca relaxed, Roy closed his hand and hit Rebecca, again catching her at her temple and left cheekbone.

"Nice watchdog. Your husband should have gotten you a German shepherd … What a good man you have. Leaves you here alone … You told him about me, right?"

Rebecca's face was throbbing.

"You're a stupid fucking bitch! Do you know how much you fucked up my life?"

"You're a stupid fucking dick! Do you know how much you're fucking up mine?"

Roy laughed. "Feisty! I bet you don't show your perfect husband Jack that side of you."

Rebecca's anger grew. How could this guy be in her house in her life after all this time? How was this even possible? Why wasn't she strong enough, smart enough to keep this from happening?

"Maybe I'll take what I should have had a long time ago." He reached over and grabbed her breast."

Rebecca punched him as hard as she could in the mouth.

Roy slapped her again in the same place across the left side of the face. When she turned back to look at him, she noticed a cut on his lip.

Rebecca's tough eastside past was still with her. And she was thankful. Her best friends Cecilia and Rachael were right there with her, ready to fight. Vicki, Renae and Lupe were yelling at Rebecca to stay strong. Her new friends were with her, too: Angie, Leslie and Christy were in her corner. Rebecca was channeling all these incredible women into herself. She would win this and survive. Together, they would take care of Roy. He didn't stand a chance.

Knowing this battle couldn't be won physically, she had to use her brain. She knew she couldn't rely on the alarm system or the telephone. What about her cell phone? Was he able to tamper with her cell phone that was on the dresser not far from her? She went over everything she learned in self-defense. What did she have for a weapon on her night stand: clock, phone, lamp, pen? Maybe she could stick the pen into his eye. If she was able to push it in far enough, she might kill him.

Surprising herself that she could even consider killing somebody. She'd never want to live with that guilt, she thought, then wondered why have compassion for somebody who continued hurting her? Was she missing a gene? Were most women missing that gene? If her friends were there, would they kill him for her? Roy might kill her … If he kills her, it would be too late for her to kill him first.

Hearing Lily whimper, Rebecca convinced herself that Lily was safe and Jack was safe, as long as he didn't come home early. So Rebecca had one person to worry about, one person to protect—herself.

The blood started to run from Roy's lip. He touched the drop with his fingers. "Good hit, but you're so fucked up right now. You have no idea how bad you look. You're so ugly, I'll have to cover your face when I fuck you."

Rebecca cringed.

He grabbed Rebecca's hand and pressed it against his hard penis. "In time, my angel."

She pulled her hand away. Should she pretend she liked him, wanted to be back with him. Should she badmouth Jack? "Remember when you sang "Blue Eyes" to me?"

"If I was going to sing it to you now, I'd have to sing "Blue Eye," he laughed. "Get it? You only have one eye."

"I think I'm having a bad dream. You're not really here."

"Yes, I am."

"No, I don't think so. I'll wake up tomorrow and everything will be fine. You'll be checking in with your parole officer."

"You're fucking with me."

"No, I'm not, it's your dream too. Why'd you dream this? What do you want?"

Lily barked, then started whimpering.

"Why would I have a stupid fuckin' dog in my dream?" He struck her again.

His insanity scared her, but she pretended everything was fine. "Well, I'm going to get up and make some coffee. Do you want some?" She lifted the covers in hopes of getting him off her bed so she could get up and run for her cell. As she held the covers, he grabbed her arm and forced it behind her back. She was sure her shoulder would come out of the socket. He forced her back down on the bed on her stomach. He was on top of her and tried to pull down her pajama bottoms. The pajama string was tied tightly around her waist and her bottoms wouldn't pull down. Her arm felt like it would break from him pressing against her, forcefully thrusting against her back. He kept trying to remove her pants. She could feel the burn of the fabric cutting into her hips.

He moaned and went still.

Rebecca knew he'd ejaculated but couldn't tell if his pants were down or not. She didn't feel anything wet. Rebecca was filled with fear, and she fought tears. He was so much stronger than she was. If her pants had come down … the thought made her nauseous. Her shoulder was throbbing, and she didn't know if it was still in place or broken or torn.

She wasn't sure if it was from the pain or what had just happened, but her mouth started watering and, before she knew it, she was vomiting. Roy stood up quickly and started pacing back and forth in her bedroom.

Rebecca slid her right arm down her back. The pain was excruciating. She hoped the hurting would stop. As her arm passed down the backside of her body, she felt nothing wet on her back or butt. His jeans had still been on.

"Get up!" he yelled.

She did.

He grabbed her same arm and forced it behind her back and pushed her as they walked down the hall and down the stairs. She could hear Lily whining and barking. She was now far from her cell phone.

As they got to the foot of the stairs, Rebecca saw the bookcase she had wanted to move with its two solid glass sculptures: the wolf and the bear. They were heavy, but small enough that she could lift them and possibly use one as a weapon.

But not now, not the way he had her shoulder. He told her to turn on the lights and close the blinds that faced the driveway. She did as she was told. After she set the remote down, he shoved her onto the couch. Her shoulder throbbed as her arm straightened.

"I need a drink of water," Rebecca said, still tasting the vomit in her mouth.

Roy ignored her and sat on the edge of a chair facing her.

She could see the front of his pants were wet, and she almost vomited again. The hitting hadn't weakened her as much as the attempted rape and his strength. She felt defeated. She knew he would try again. She started to believe he was going to kill her. One way or another, she would lose at least a part of herself if not her whole life before this was over.

"You are so fuckin' ugly right now," he said staring at her. "You have puke on your face." He laughed, shaking his head. "I got beat up in prison, but I never looked as bad as you look. I think I broke your cheekbone. You're fragile. You act tough, but you're fragile." He leaned in to touch her face.

Rebecca punched him on the mouth again.

Roy slapped her on the same side of her face as before.

Rebecca turned her head back to face him and started to cry. Tears were pouring from both eyes. She was broken. She was in so much pain, her shoulder, her face. Her hand hurt from hitting him and her head was pounding. The tears were stinging her eyes.

"Oh, now you're going to cry! Fuckin' baby! Waa. Waa."

"Why are you doing this?"

"You put me in prison!"

"You put yourself in prison! It's illegal to stalk and beat up people."

"I didn't beat you up!"

"I had to go to the hospital. I have permanent hearing damage. Yes, you beat me up."

"I did not. I hardly even touched you!"

She knew all abusers minimize the abuse they inflict on others. "I didn't press charges, the state did. Why don't you go harass the state?"

Roy lifted his hand to hit her again but didn't.

Rebecca was thankful. "You served your time; why don't you just go and get on with your life?"

"What life? I'm a felon because of you," he said, pretending he was going to hit her again.

Rebecca flinched.

He raised his hand once more to scare her.

She flinched again.

"Maybe I should find a career in dishwashing."

"Or your music, or you can get on some medication and start helping others …"

"Shut up! Fuck!" He covered his ears like a five year old who didn't want to listen.

Rebecca had quit crying and she felt her strength coming back to her: Cecilia, Rachel, Vicki, Angie and Leslie were all back with her.

What were her options? Her cell phone was upstairs. Her car was in the garage. Those glass pieces were behind her to her left. If she lived in town, she could just take off out the front door and run to the street or a neighbors. But here she had no place to run.

There were knives in the kitchen, but she didn't trust herself to keep them away from Roy. She didn't want to give him any ideas. As far as she could tell he had no weapons: just his own strength and his hands. That was one thing she had going for her. And he hadn't tied her up. But he did have a small black backpack he was carrying with him.

"How'd you meet this Jack guy?"

Rebecca ignored his question.

Roy kneeled down by Rebecca and lifted her shirt to see her breasts. He grabbed the string on her pajamas bottoms and pulled the string loose. He stood back up and began pacing in front of her.

"I know the reason you didn't press charges or testify or whatever you didn't do, was because you were with Jack. If you hadn't been with Jack you would have tried to put me away for longer. I probably would have gotten more time. The best witness didn't show, or should I say the person who wanted to see me suffer the most, revenge or something. You didn't show up. My lawyer told me that in the beginning you were there in court. I guess I should be glad you're with Jack. But I'm not. You should have waited for me."

Rebecca knew better than to argue with his delusions.

"You know while I was on the run, I broke into my uncle's place and stole a pistol? I got desperate. I was broke, hungry and nobody would help me out. I held up two convenience stores. That's how they caught up with me. I wasn't going to shoot anybody; I just needed some money. They were so stupid ... crying, scared pussy. They had a fuckin' camera." He slapped Rebecca across the face.

She kept her eyes closed until the stinging softened.

"It's your fault ... see what you did to me, what you turned me into?"

She wondered when Jack would call if the phone would ring busy or continue ringing like nobody was home. When would he call the police? How long would it take? Or would Jack do anything at all? If he tried to call her cell, would she be able to run upstairs and answer his call and tell him to call the police? She doubted she could get to her phone in time.

Rebecca glanced at the clock; it was almost three thirty. She couldn't depend on Jack—she had to depend on herself, and she had one chance. She would not risk something she wasn't sure about, like hitting the panic button on the alarm system that probably didn't work or trying to run upstairs to get her cell. If she tried something and failed, he'd tie her up or worse.

"You know, I think I want you to take your clothes off."

"No."

"Yes, I think I do. You fucked with me so much during our relationship."

"Jack's on his way home."

"Yes, but not until tonight. We have time. Don't worry."

"He's coming home early, this morning. He told me last night when he called," Rebecca lied. "Just tell me what you want. Do you want me to tell you I'm sorry?" she asked. "I'm sorry. I'm sorry for everything. I'm sorry if I hurt you. I'm sorry you had to go to jail …"

"It wasn't jail! It was prison!"

"I'm sorry you had to go to prison! But what about me? Are you sorry? Are you sorry for what you put me through?"

Roy mule kicked at Rebecca and caught her in the upper chest. She heard a pop sound. He knocked the wind out of her. She fell back and onto her side, her eyes closed in pain. She couldn't breathe.

Surprisingly, Roy knelt down by the couch to check on her. While gasping for air, she refused to open her eyes. She was sure something broke on her left side, maybe her clavicle. Rebecca was in excruciating pain. She knew she would not speak another word to Roy.

Rebecca felt defeated and weak. She didn't know how she would be able to defend herself or fight back. She started believing that Roy had won. He had won a long time ago because she would be afraid for the rest of her life.

She started to cry again. She had had every opportunity to get a body-guard or do some further checking. She could have called Roy's parole officer and called Victim Services again. Why did she stay in denial? Why did she think she could handle it by herself? She could have reminded Jack that Roy had been released. She should have called the sheriff's department. Who cared if she sounded crazy? Why did she convince herself that he wouldn't come after her? Why wasn't she smarter?

Rebecca was sure it was her collarbone that was broken. She didn't know how she would be able to use her arm without agony. It was the same shoulder Roy had been torturing. She tried to appreciate that she still had one good arm left.

Rebecca was finally starting to breathe normally when she heard Roy say that he was sorry.

"Rebecca? Rebecca?" He gently shook her.

Rebecca kept her eyes closed and didn't respond.

"I know you can hear me … I … I love you."

Rebecca ignored Roy and wondered why she hadn't told Jack everything: the Polo, the footprint downstairs, seeing somebody on their property. She knew why. She wanted to take care of it herself. She wanted to win. She was tired of feeling that Roy had won in beating her down, making her crazy. She was stronger than that. She didn't want to depend on Jack's money or a man to keep her safe. She wanted to keep herself safe. Rebecca feared if she revealed her true worries and concerns, Jack might start thinking of her as frail and not the strong woman he married.

Rebecca had already been living in her own prison because of what Roy had done to her and the possibility of him stalking her again. But if she told Jack about being afraid of Roy, she feared he would also put her in a prison of wanting to protect her. Her home would become a prison and a bodyguard would feel like a prison guard.

Rebecca tried to move her right arm slightly to see how much pain it would cause. Miraculously, she was able to move her arm. Okay, she thought, this is good. She'd lie there a little longer.

She was afraid to talk, afraid to cry, and especially afraid to protect herself or fight for herself. She thought about the first time he attacked her. The only reason she got through it was because he made a mistake, he turned his back on her so she could run out of the apartment. It was really nothing that she did; he made the mistake. And maybe he'd make another mistake.

She couldn't talk her way out of it, she couldn't overpower him, especially in her condition, and she couldn't run to a neighbor's. Her best strategy was to wait.

Rebecca thought about every woman in her situation. The one thing that they all had in common was that the perpetrators where doing these things behind closed doors, never in public. These guys were all the same; they were all weak and cowardly.

Rebecca could feel Roy staring at her. She tried to stay as still as she could. His concern made her sick. She was surprised he didn't try to rape her again. She knew she was alive and that was all that mattered to her. Rebecca had no plans of moving until she had to.

4:08 AM

LILY STARTED BARKING as if somebody had pulled up onto the driveway. Then her cell phone started ringing upstairs. Roy panicked.

Rebecca opened her eyes and saw Roy jump up to peek through the closed blinds at the wall of windows. Rebecca jumped to her feet, grabbed the glass sculpture from the bookcase by the stairs and ran as fast as she could toward Roy. He turned toward her just as she slammed the glass wolf into his head with both arms. She caught him at the side of his head, not the back of his head where she had planned, but it seemed to be enough.

It happened so fast. The chunk of glass did not break, but as it fell to the floor blood splattered onto the beige carpet. She looked at Roy who was looking back at her, stunned. Only a small amount of blood trickled from the gash on his head. Then his eyes rolled back, and he fell to the floor stiff as a board onto his stomach. Once he hit the floor, blood gushed out of his cut, and he started bleeding profusely.

Rebecca's adrenaline kicked in. Holding her arm as if it were in a sling, she ran toward the front door, opened the closet and grabbed Lily's leash and a twenty-five foot leash that Jack had used to help train Lily.

She rushed back to Roy and started to tie him up using her knee, her mouth and her good arm, trying not to use her bad arm. She didn't want to take any chances of him waking up before the police came. She started with his hands behind his back. She wrapped the leash around his hands, then in between and back around him. She went around his waist, figure-eighting the leash. When she felt his hands were secure, she took the remainder of the leash and started tying his feet together at the ankle. She looped the end of Lily's lead through the handle of the shorter leash securely attaching the two together. She continued tying his feet.

When she was finished, she went to the kitchen and got a knife. She went back to Roy and stood over him. She didn't know if he was alive. She saw no movement, not even him breathing. She started to cry. She sat down on the floor holding the knife, rocking forward and back. She cried because she was afraid. She cried because she felt that maybe she had won the battle. She cried because she had to go through this in the first place, twice.

Who does she blame, Roy or the state or herself? The state didn't counsel him, the state let him out when they knew he was making threats to kill her. Nobody called her to warn her that he was missing, no longer checking in with his parole officer. Jack wouldn't have left town or he would have gotten her a bodyguard. Nobody contacted her or seemed to care about her, her life or her safety.

Roy came so close to raping her. Even though he didn't stick his dick in her, she still felt something deep inside that hurt badly because of what had happened. Maybe just knowing how easy it would have been for him to rape her, Rebecca became enraged.

She stood up and kicked him lifting her toes to use the ball of her foot into his side. She heard him make a slight grunt. That scared her. She double checked the security of the leashes and went upstairs to her cell phone. She sat in the closet and dialed Jack's phone.

Rebecca couldn't hold her cell phone up with her right arm. She couldn't hold the phone to the left side of her face.

"Hi, honey. I hope I didn't wake you," he said in his cheery voice. "I know it's early, but I couldn't sleep. I had strange feelings; I wanted to check on you."

Rebecca listened to him talk, but she didn't understand what he was saying.

"Reb, I tried the home phone, but it just kept ringing. That's why I called your cell. Are you at home? ... Are you okay?"

"Jack?"

"Yes, it's Jack."

Rebecca started to cry.

"Rebecca!"

"Roy is here ... I hit him and I think he's going to die."

"Roy who ... Oh, my God! Reb, are you okay? Oh, my God! I'll call the police!"

"No don't! I don't ... I don't want anybody here right now!"

She heard Jack crying.

"I think I'm going to kill him or wait for him to die before I call the police."

"Reb, what happened? What did he do to you!"

Jack's high pitched cry made Rebecca cry harder.

"Reb!" he sobbed ... "What did he do to you? ... What did he do to you?"

Rebecca just kept crying into the phone. She said nothing.

Jack kept crying. "Oh, God, Rebecca. I'm so sorry ... I'm so sorry ... I'll be right there. I'll get a plane ... I'll be right there." He hung up.

She knew he would call the police.

She kept crying into the phone even though Jack was no longer there. She wanted Roy to die. She didn't want to go through this a third time. She could go and kill him right now before the police came.

She knew that once the police were there, they would start doing CPR on Roy. They would do whatever they could to try to save his life. She knew that he would look like the victim. She figured that the male police officers would be taken aback. They wouldn't want to see a man as a victim; they would expect to see the woman as the victim.

Rebecca went back downstairs and into her office to check on Lily; she was fine. Rebecca left Lily locked in the room. She sat on the floor looking at Roy. Blood was everywhere. She knew she couldn't kill him, but she prayed that he would die.

After a few minutes, she heard the sirens. She walked over and unlocked and opened the front door. The alarm didn't go off. She waited outside as police and ambulance medics filled the house.

Rebecca sat alone on the front step. She didn't want to watch the EMTs save Roy's life, so she watched the sheriffs talk and compare notes. She looked out to the hillside and wondered if the coyotes were watching. She shivered in the cool night, waiting for somebody to talk to her.

After a female officer showed up, two other deputies joined her in questioning Rebecca. She answered their questions and watched the commotion inside the house.

The medics covered Roy with a sheet. It was over. Roy was dead.

Rebecca's eyes filled with tears, and she couldn't hide her smile.

About the Author

Becky Due is the new voice of women's fiction. She has the courage, honesty and writing style for today's busy women, and she does not cringe away from hard issues. She will leave you feeling strong, self-confident, independent, and in control of your life.

Her books have won and been finalists in several independent competitions including the 2010 and 2011 National Indie Excellence Awards, USA Book News and the 2009 IPPY Awards.

Other Great Titles by Becky Due

The Gentlemen's Club: A Story for All Women (Novel)

Touchable Love: An Untraditional Love Story (Novel)

Returning Injury: A Suspense Celebrating Women's Strength (Novel)

The Dumpster: One Woman's Search for Love (Novel)

Traveling for Love: Searching for Self, Hoping for Love (Novel)

Blue the Bird: On Flying (Children's)

The Woman's Handbook: Everything You Want To Say To Your Daughter, Sister, Niece, Friend In One Simple Book (Gift Book/Self-Help)

2 Days to Healthy Self-Esteem (Self-Help)

I'm Upset! App for Women (App)

Visit Becky Due at

http://www.BeckyDue.com
http://www.facebook.com/BeckyDue.Author
http://www.twitter.com/BeckyDue